Misterioso

Also by Alan Plater
available from Methuen

The Beiderbecke Affair
The Beiderbecke Tapes

ALAN PLATER

Misterioso

Methuen

First published in Great Britain 1987
by Methuen London Ltd
11 New Fetter Lane, London EC4P 4EE

Copyright © 1987 by Alan Plater

Printed and bound in Great Britain
by Redwood Burn Ltd,
Trowbridge, Wilts

British Library Cataloguing in Publication Data

Plater, Alan
Misterioso.
I. Title
823'.914 [F]   PR6066.L3
ISBN 0-413-15380-0

The book is dedicated to Rachel

Author's Note

In writing *Misterioso*, I have drawn extensively on official and unofficial jazz history – the music, the players and singers, the anecdotes and one-liners. I have given credit within the text wherever possible to Thelonious Monk, Duke Ellington, Ronnie Scott and the other cats in the band; but I'd like to add a general thank you, lightly and politely, to all those jazz people who have helped me make this book, even if they don't realize it.

CONTENTS

ONE

Misterioso

Said the dark-haired man: ' "Misterioso"? It's a piece of music. A blues, naturally, like all my best friends. Written by Thelonious Monk. Piano player, full name – Thelonious Sphere Monk. If you're a musician, you'll understand me when I say it's a blues built around walking sixths. If you're not a musician, let me offer my congratulations and tell you "Misterioso" is a tune that haunts you. Always beyond reach. Just around the corner. A sweet promise and the echo of a sad dream.'

He smiled, mostly at himself.

'Yes, well, sure, so that's all a load of pretentious crap. But you did ask the question.'

TWO

All Blues

You don't see many pretty, well-dressed girls hanging around car dumps. That was Tom's experience, and he had been hanging around dumps most of his working life. Now, at the age of fifty, he had his own dump plus a detached house and beer belly, all three paid for.

The motor car was his best friend. It was a fact of life that every car that ever rolled off an assembly line, apart from the few eccentric survivors that made the London-to-Brighton once a year, ended up broken, rotting, neglected and redundant. Every technological miracle inflicted on the human race resulted in more scrap metal, despite the manufacturers' guarantees. The knowledge gave Tom much comfort and had educated his children.

Most of his days he worked alone, dissecting bodywork and chassis, recycling the scrap metal back into the great system. The solitude gave ample time for contented brooding; you are never alone with your garbage.

The girl was pretty, in her mid-twenties, with dark, serious, questing eyes and a face touching sadness.

Tom called to her: 'Are you looking for something, flower?'

She walked across to him, treading carefully among the wreckage, but without fear.

'Yes, I'm looking for something.'

'Like what, for instance?'

'A car.'

Tom's immediate response was to smile. He always smiled easily. Wandering into his empire in search of a car was akin to calling on Battersea Dogs' Home hoping to hear a bark. He would have laughed out loud but something behind the girl's eyes told him not to.

'A car?' he confirmed gently, playing for time.

'Yes.'

Together they scanned the immediate horizons. There was nothing to be seen but the last remains of cars, nestling in coarse grass, shrouded by a grey northern sky.

'If it's a car you're looking for, you've come to the right place, love,' said Tom, 'unless you're wanting to drive off in it. Wouldn't fancy your chances of doing that. Or is it a spare part you're after?'

'None of those things. I want to look at the car that killed my mother.'

On the night – and for the rest of her life it would always be 'the night' – Rachel had not been allowed to look, though she had tried.

'I want to go and look.'

'No.'

And Will had grabbed her, tightly, by the wrist.

'But I *want* to!'

'No.'

One hand grasped her wrist, the other on her shoulder and the restraint turned into an embrace, then, more simply, into the cuddle given to a child at Christmas when the batteries run down on the favourite toy.

Over Will's shoulder she could see the car skewed across the road, wedged under the cab of the oil tanker. All around were flashing lights: from fire engine, ambulance and police cars. It reminded her of so many accident scenes in television cop shows. Mum's dead, she thought, and it's just another episode in just another series.

It was her first encounter with death in adult life and the elements were just too ordinary: a PTA meeting, a wet road, a skid, a telephone call, a policeman's tentative words:

'I'm afraid there's been an accident . . .'

Perhaps this was the usual way of death: ordinary. Perhaps we had all been brainwashed by Shakespeare and his like. We had all been promised heroic nobility, a stoical journey to the inevitable, with flights of angels to ease the passing. Instead of which Rachel had moved through a

3

mumbled message from a nervous policeman to a cuddle from Will under the flashing blue light.

She was crying, of course; but she found herself smiling at the same time, again like a child at Christmas.

Will noticed the smile. That was his way. He noticed everything.

'What is it?'

'I've known you for five years, and lived with you for two. But I didn't realize you were strong.'

'I'm not,' said Will.

Rachel and Tom looked at the car, a four-year-old Volkswagen with a crumpled bonnet. There was no glass in the windscreen, no door at the driver's side.

'Is that it?' said Tom.

'That's it.'

'Was your mother driving?'

'Yes.'

She took a closer look at the car, concentrating on the driver's seat, visualizing coldly, without public emotion, the precise mechanics of death.

'What happened?'

'She collided with an oil tanker. It was overtaking a van from the other direction. The police said he was in the wrong. Still – right or wrong – what difference?'

'The difference is he'll lose his licence and his job.'

She nodded, acknowledging the man's sense of rough justice.

'Thank you for letting me see.'

'Any time, love.'

Rachel turned, started to walk away, then hesitated. She felt comfortable talking to a stranger. Families stood too close, and knew too much. Besides, the man deserved an explanation.

'On the night, they wouldn't let me see it. Scared it would upset me. I'm only a woman, you see. Not strong.'

'That's a load of bollocks an' all,' said Tom, then apologized immediately: 'Excuse the language.'

'It's OK.'

4

'But it is.'

'A load of bollocks?'

Tom nodded. 'About women not being strong, yes it is. I could tell you things . . .'

The words tailed off. He could have told her things about his father, killed in Burma, and his mother, bringing up a family on a widow's pension and a prayer, but this was neither the time nor the place and the girl had burdens enough to carry. He only knew that women were strong, stronger than men, and it was the girl who needed to talk and find her strength.

'Was there anybody else in the car? On the night?'

'Yes. My father.'

'How's my father?'

She had visited John in hospital, before driving to the car dump. She took refuge in a traditional opening greeting honed down the years. He responded, playing the same game.

'All the better for seeing you, my dear.'

'Good.'

Then the game stopped.

'How was the funeral?'

He had been too ill to attend. He had protested that broken ribs and concussion were minor problems but he knew he protested too much. The doctors knew it, too, and so did the family.

Rachel shrugged.

'It was . . . like a funeral. You know funerals. We all cried a lot. Then, afterwards, we laughed a little bit. I think Grandma enjoyed it.'

'She probably did.'

'I wasn't crazy about the vicar.'

'He's always been a good friend to the school. Comes to speech days. Scatters a few bromides. Besides, your mother was a card-carrying atheist. You can't expect miracles.'

He lay back on the pillow. It was the longest speech he had made since the night of the accident, and the first time

5

he had attempted the sometimes self-conscious jauntiness they both enjoyed.

Rachel tried to sustain the mood: 'It was busy at the crematorium. One every fifteen minutes.'

'Must be the time of year. I suppose it's all seasonal.'

They were trying hard; but it was all very well for John Donne to say Death, be not proud, and for sweet sad Dylan to rage about not going gentle. Father and daughter had both discovered it was not a good night, and the days that followed were even worse. It was time to own up.

'I don't know how I'm going to live without her,' said John.

'Neither do I. But we will.'

John held out a hand. Rachel laid hers upon it.

'Will you do something for me?'

'Sure.'

'Will you sort through the papers? The documents. Insurances. All the bullshit that proves somebody exists . . .'

Then he cried, a quiet grief that stretched back a quarter of a century and perhaps beyond. Rachel stood up and kissed him on the top of his head. That, too, was part of their tradition, dating back to the historic moment when his bald patch first became visible to the naked eye.

'I'll see to everything, Dad. And I love you.'

He nodded.

'I know,' he said, but the words were scarcely audible.

Tom walked her towards the exit, along an avenue formed by wrecked cars. It was like walking down the aisle at the crematorium.

'Have you got much of a family?' asked Tom.

'My Dad and a young sister.'

'Do you live at home? Or are you married?' Then he back-tracked: 'Sorry. I should mind my own bloody business.'

She smiled, reassuring.

'It doesn't matter. I've got nothing to be ashamed of.'

'Hard luck, flower. Maybe things'll pick up.'

'I live with my bloke.'

'Oh aye. There's a lot do it these days. Helps the tax, doesn't it?'

'Helps the divorce rate an' all.'

She felt sufficiently confident to echo, discreetly, his Yorkshire accent.

They reached the end of the avenue, and the exit from the dump. Its boundary was a healthy, old-fashioned hedgerow. He noticed her approving glance.

'Good hedge, isn't it? People keep wanting me to tear it up, but I tell them: there's mice and rats and all sorts of creepy-crawlies live in there. Doing my bit for conservation. I'm just a peasant.'

'What's wrong with that?'

'I didn't say there was anything wrong with it.'

She opened her handbag, looked for her car keys, found them with the usual difficulty.

'Thank you for letting me see . . .'

He knew she didn't want to say the words and came to her rescue. 'Any time you fancy a browse through my scrap metal, you're more than welcome.'

'It was good to talk. Funny how you can talk to strangers about . . .'

Again he came to her rescue, though maybe it wasn't necessary.

'About death?'

'Yes.'

'I was the same when my dog died. Talking to everybody. Total strangers. In the pub, in shops, at the match. And I cried buckets. Big strong man. Car wrecker. Cried buckets.'

'I can imagine that.' She unlocked the door of the car. 'What sort of dog was it?'

'Cocker spaniel. But it still pains me to think about him.'

He turned, quite abruptly, and walked back into his wasteland. As Rachel drove away, she could hear the harsh whine of a mechanical saw, attacking metal.

* * *

She sat at the dining table, with the documentation arranged before her in orderly sequence: birth certificate, O and A level certificates, marriage certificate, wedding photographs, programmes for school concerts, insurance policies, holiday postcards from people she could not clearly identify. When Will arrived with the coffee, she had to clear a space.

'Are you winning?' he asked.

'It isn't a game.'

Will sat down opposite her, and browsed through a shoebox filled with snapshots. Rachel leaned back in her chair, stretching and relaxing her shoulders. Her neck ached.

'It seems like an insult.'

'What does?'

'All this stuff. Tie it up with pink ribbon. Stick it in a cupboard. That's my mother's life disposed of. Is that it? Is that the lot?'

'Of course not. That's just the bits of paper. It's everything else she left behind. You and Dawn and your Dad, and all the good times you had. They were good times, weren't they?'

It was rhetorical. He knew the family had shared good times, because Rachel had told him so, often. In the last few years he had been part of them, and could bear witness.

'You never really know your parents, do you?'

She drank a little of her coffee. The mug — they always drank from mugs except when her grandparents visited — bore the word Peace in several languages. Will's mug was from the Railway Museum. Their icons popped up all over the flat: Picasso's Dove on the chimney breast, Humphrey Bogart in the bedroom, Emma Goldman in the entrance hall, York City FC in the lavatory.

'I know a few facts, that's all.'

'Start with the facts and work outwards,' said Will.

She slid a notepad from beneath a thin layer of bank statements and holiday guides.

'I've been making a list. Date of birth. School career.

Examination passes. University graduation. Date of marriage. When she passed her driving test. My birth. Dawn's birth. Holiday in Crete. Holiday in Florence. Weekend conference in Scotland on urban renewal. See? I didn't know she was into urban renewal.'

'She planted a tree once. In plant-a-tree year. That one in the back garden. It has pink flowers on it. Sometimes.'

'So that's urban renewal we've pinned down. And trees. But what about the rest? Did she ever want to scream? Did she really love my Dad? Was she faithful to him? If so, why? If not, why not?'

'Are there any love letters?'

'No. Plenty of bank statements. She had more money than I thought. Not what you'd call a lot of money but . . .'

'Rachel.'

He spoke firmly, by his standards, tenderly by those of the go-getting late twentieth century.

'What?'

'Will you marry me?'

'Huh?'

He had asked the question before. It generally came round about once a month. This time, oddly, it took her by surprise, but the answer was the same as on previous occasions.

'No, I don't think so.'

'Why not?'

'We've been living together peacefully for a couple of years. We have good times. Why spoil it with confetti and ham salads? Unless you're pregnant.'

'I'm serious.'

She looked at him across the table, knowing exactly what she would see: an open face, totally without guile. His smile could be like the sunrise. When he was serious, as now, there was an innocence and a sadness as old as time. At these moments he reminded her of Buster Keaton, the most beautiful man who ever lived.

'You're a nice man, Will. And a gentle man and

9

beautiful to live with. But we're much too young to be doing daft things like getting married.'

'Too young! We're twenty-six! We should be having babies.'

'Twenty-six is young.'

Will got up from the table, and crossed to the built-in unit he had designed and made to house their record collection.

'Mahler?' she said.

It was one of their continuing jokes. When he was happy, he played Mozart, Erik Satie, Fats Domino, Spike Jones and the City Slickers; when he was unhappy, he played Mahler. It seemed to Rachel that so many relationships were built around jokes and quirkiness of this kind, like the affectionate one-liners she shared with her father. It would make a good examination question. Life is a series of interlocking running gags: discuss, quoting relevant examples.

She had guessed right. Will took Mahler's Sixth Symphony from the shelf, slid the record from its sleeve.

'Save the music and talk to me.' She got up in her turn and crossed to him, putting an arm around his shoulder. 'Talk to me, Will.'

He tried.

'I suppose I thought if we got married it would sort of counter-balance your mother. In the midst of death we are in life. That sort of thing.'

'Ensure the continuity of the human species?'

'It isn't a joke!'

Again the upraised voice, twice in an evening now, frustration dressed in yearning.

'I know it isn't a joke, love. If I thought it was all a joke, I'd marry you tomorrow. I'd even cross my fingers and do it in a church. Race you down the aisle and the last one to the altar pays the choirboys. But . . .'

She slowly removed her arm from around his shoulder.

'I'm sorry, Will. Play the music.'

She returned to her place at the table, and her task of excavating a life. Will played his music.

* * *

Later, in bed, they made love, and then Rachel tried to explain.

'Let me hit you with a confession. I did not really know my mother.'

'You said all that. You didn't know she was into urban renewal and you can't tell whether she was faithful to your Dad or whether she wanted to scream. And because of that you refuse my very reasonable offer.'

As often, Will startled her with his ability and, for that matter, his concern to listen to her words over a period of time, and remember them. In her experience, very few people really listened to anybody, and sure as hell, they didn't remember much afterwards. Will was different, and for that she treasured him.

Patiently, she tried again to explain.

'Tonight I discovered the proof that I did not really know my mother.'

'Perhaps you'd like to tell your story to the court.'

'I checked their marriage certificate against my birth certificate. They *had* to get married. Like the book says ... I was conceived out of wedlock. I could have been a real bastard, if Dad hadn't done the decent thing.'

'There might have been a shotgun sticking in his back. Anyway, what's it matter? People having to get married ... it's no big deal.'

Bogey looked down on them from his prime position overlooking the bed. He had obviously seen it all before, all the big deals both in and out of wedlock.

'It doesn't bother me,' said Rachel. 'What bothers me is they didn't *tell* me. If they didn't tell me that, what else didn't they tell me? And if I don't really know my parents, how can I possibly know myself? And if I don't know myself, how can I possibly get married? Even to a sweet guy like you? Especially to a sweet guy like you?'

'Not only that, I'm a good cook.'

He turned over on his side, facing away from Rachel. It was not a hostile gesture, but a friendly and familiar signal that he wanted to go to sleep. She kissed him on the back of the neck, noticed his hair needed cutting then turned over on her front. She had read in a colour supplement years ago that this was a healthy way to sleep. She had never had a serious illness, so maybe it worked.

'Sleep tight,' she said.

'Don't go too near the edge,' he replied.

It was their nightly ritual. Another examination question. Life is a complex of endearing rituals and half-truths: discuss, quoting examples.

Her father left hospital a week later. She went with her sister to bring him home. Dawn had struck a deal, with the cool assurance of a sixteen-year-old with nine O levels and Oxbridge beckoning – probably in vain – on her horizon.

'You do the driving, I'll do the cheerful chat.'

Dawn sat in the back of the two-door Fiat and, as usual, added mobility to the act of sitting, bobbing forward at what seemed like fifteen-second intervals, nestling between Rachel and her father.

'Does it still hurt when you laugh, Dad?'

'I don't know yet.'

He was trying hard to enter into the spirit of rebuilding, but it was difficult. It was his first time in a car since the night of the accident.

'I've been collecting these really fabulous jokes from school, and saving them up for when you come out of hospital, and this is the day we've all been waiting for.'

'Do you ever try breathing while you speak?' asked Rachel.

'Don't be a misery, I've got this great joke to tell Dad. There was an Englishman, an Irishman, a Scotsman and an orang-utan and they all went into this discotheque in Leeds . . .'

Rachel glanced across at her father's face.

'Can we save the jokes for another time?' she said, quickly.

'Suit yourself. I'm just honouring my contract to supply cheerful conversation with a hint of controversy.' She switched her attention to John. 'Trouble is, Dad, she just

12

wants to talk about dead serious things all the time.'

'What sort of dead serious things?'

'Pass.'

The house lay in the commuter suburbs to the west of York. Once upon a mediaeval time there had been a village, with a pond and annual muck-spreading, but in the twentieth century absentee farmers discovered semi-detached bungalows were a more profitable crop than grain. The pub served ploughman's lunches of a kind never seen in a field, let alone within spitting distance of a plough.

Will had left work early to prepare a meal for the hospital party. He lifted the lid from a large casserole, revealing one of his celebrated baked pastas.

'Just a little for me,' said Rachel and her father, more or less in unison.

'Just a lot for me,' said Dawn, who had an enduring affection for food, and for Will. She called him her *de facto* brother-in-law. 'It looks terrific,' she said, as she started her assault on the food.

'It is,' said Will. 'On the packet it says – guaranteed terrific, or your money refunded.'

'Why don't you marry this bloke, our kid? He's great.'

'I'm thinking about it,' said Rachel.

'Thinking about it? Has he asked you?'

Rachel did not reply. Dawn was not a girl to take no answer for an answer. She moved the point of attack to Will.

'Have you asked her? Have you done the full kneeling bit?'

'Several times.'

Dawn was indignant. 'And she said No?'

Will nodded. Dawn turned on Rachel with a calculated display of spontaneous outrage.

'You said No? You want your brains washing. I'd marry him tomorrow if he asked me. I mean, look at this . . .'

She indicated the rapidly diminishing heap of pasta on her plate.

'And he's good-looking, well, fairly good-looking, and

13

he's got a steady job, and he laughs at my fabulous jokes.'

'I'll bear it in mind,' said Will. Then he turned to John. They were all aware of his silence in the surrounding banter. Saying nothing, he was making more noise than any of them.

'Is it good to be home?' Will asked him.

'It's good . . .' He hesitated, as if trying to think of something good, then continued: '. . . to be out of hospital.'

He said no more. Dawn, abhorring any combination of silence or stillness, chipped in speedily: 'And it must be good to be back in the bosom of your family. That's got to be special, hasn't it? I mean, I realize Rachel and Will are only passing through and therefore the family consists of me, but I'm all I've got and I promise not to tell too many of my fabulous jokes.'

John stopped eating and got up from his place at the table.

'I'm sorry, Will. This is delicious but I don't feel very hungry. You three carry on.'

He walked through into the kitchen. Then they heard the back door open and close.

'You know what you do, don't you?' said Rachel to her sister.

'Talk too much?'

'Right.'

'Somebody's got to try to be cheerful and chatty. You can go off to the flat and be all soulful with Will. I've got to go on living here with Dad. Just because I talk a lot, it doesn't mean I don't cry a lot as well.'

No longer the omniscient teenager, she was a very young girl at bay, needing someone to hold her. Rachel knew the symptoms. She stood, walked round behind Dawn's chair, put her arms round her neck and gave her a big hug.

'I expect Dad'll be in the greenhouse, waiting for some proper grown-up talk,' said Dawn.

'I expect so.'

She kissed the top of Dawn's head, then walked into the

14

kitchen. Again there was the sound of the back door as it opened, then closed.

'I love jolly family parties, don't you, Will?'

'My favourite.'

'We only need my Grandma here and we could have a real bloodbath.'

'Yes, she's rather good at rows, isn't she?'

'Amazing. All right if I have seconds?'

Taking his permission for granted, Dawn served herself another large heap of pasta. Retrospectively, and smiling, Will said: 'Why don't you help yourself?'

They both laughed, easy in their friendship, secure in its well-defined boundaries. Mutual adoration of their kind worked better either side of a low fence.

Dawn, in any case, was generous with her adoration, especially of her amazing Grandma.

'She was hysterically funny at the funeral. Well, not at the funeral, at the party afterwards. She had a right go at this bloke, college lecturer, friend of Dad's. He's an expert on the Second World War. Writing a book about it. She told him he knew nothing.' She slid into a parody of a Yorkshire accent. 'We lived through it, young man, before you were born. Me in the air-raid shelter and my husband in the desert with Monty.'

'Did she convince him?'

'Sent him dashing back to the campus to rewrite chapter ten. And I'll tell you another secret.'

'What?'

'We're going to be living on your bloody pasta for the next three weeks.'

The greenhouse was at the bottom of the garden, built against the side of the garage, placed to catch the sun. Rachel's parents had built it, from self-assembly units, in the early years of their marriage, and it had housed tomato plants, chrysanthemums, a failed grape vine, a pair of rabbits called Ella and Louis, and a tortoise called Chico. This was at Dawn's insistence. She said Groucho had become a cliché – people gave his name to everything from

15

wine bars to gerbils. Besides, Chico was her favourite Marx brother. In her view, Harpo played too hard for sympathy, Groucho pretended to be wicked, but Chico was obviously wicked to the last slice. She liked that.

The greenhouse had room for two, seated on upturned boxes. For a quarter of a century it had served as a family confessional. Here each daughter, in her time, had sought comfort from mother or father with each passing crisis: an examination failed, a boyfriend betrayed, the death of a rabbit, the disappearance of Chico . . .

'But Dad!' Dawn had cried in her despair, 'a tortoise *can't* run away!'

Here, too, mother and father had shared secrets, affirmed their love and once even consummated it, in huge and prickly discomfort. At other times, the two sisters had compared notes, quoting examples, on men, women, sex, capitalism and the human condition, sometimes all in the same Sunday afternoon.

Now, on a grey autumn evening, it was John's turn to seek comfort. Rachel's turn to be the daughter-confessor.

'I wanted to be out of hospital. Everybody wants to be out of hospital. But I dreaded coming home because I knew she wouldn't be here. I expected it to be awful. The silences. The empty chair. The wrong person at the cooker. You'd moved a lot of her things so as not to upset me. Thank you for that. But still, I expected it to be awful. And it was even worse than I expected.'

'It'll get better. This was bound to be the worst day.'

'That's what everybody tells me.'

She had noticed John had been biting his nails. It was a habit he had conquered at least ten years earlier, under intense and loving pressure from the three of them. It was not a good time to refer to it.

'Can you cope with straight questions, Dad?'

'I've no idea. You can only try me and take the chance that I'll start crying again.'

'Is it better if we talk about Mum? Or is it better if we don't?'

'I don't even know that. Part of me wants to talk about

her all the time. Part of me says no, please don't. But I'm terrified that I'll wake up one day, maybe tomorrow, and I won't be able to remember the sound of her voice. I can remember it now, quite easily. But perhaps tomorrow I'll forget. God, that would be awful. I'd feel ashamed.'

'Another question.'

'Go on.'

He was talking now, and her knowledge of therapy, though sparse, included the idea that talking was better than not talking.

'I was checking the papers and documents, like you asked me. And I may not be all that brilliant at arithmetic, but according to my sums, Mum was already pregnant when you got married.'

'Yes, she was. We . . . had to get married. Well, no, we didn't *have* to. There were other solutions. We *wanted* to get married. That's the only thing you need to know, love. We *wanted* to get married.'

'Why didn't you tell me?'

'Is it important? Does it matter?'

She wanted to say yes, it's important, because it leaves questions unanswered about my mother, all the questions I didn't ask because I didn't know she was going to die, and now you're the only one who can tell me and . . .

'No more questions, please. It's still only my first day. My first real day.'

He had retreated again, inside his pain.

Dawn pushed open the door of the greenhouse.

'There's a layer of ice forming over the pasta, but if you want some pudding, there's still time.'

After they had washed up, Dawn suggested a game of Scrabble. John said he would rather sit quietly and read. Rachel said she would read, too, out of a confused sense that somehow this would keep him company.

Dawn and Will played Scrabble. Rachel pretended to read the previous week's *New Statesman*, aware that her father was not reading but digging around on the record shelves. He seemed to be looking for something, but without any certainty of purpose. The signals indicated help was not required.

But help *was* required at the Scrabble game. Will called out: 'Referee!'

Rachel, relieved to be given a role in the proceedings – any role – crossed to the table.

'Tell her she can't put that,' said Will.

Rachel looked at the words on the board.

'You wicked sinful child!'

'I'm not wicked and sinful. That's a legitimate word.'

'Explain yourself, child.'

Dawn explained, with the patience of impatient youth.

'A knacker is a man who slaughters horses. Therefore two men who slaughter horses are called knackers. If I had an "i" in my hand I could change it to knickers, but I haven't so it'll have to stay. Sorry, Will. Sorry, referee. It's knackers to both of you.'

'Send her off, ref!' said Will.

Before the dispute could be resolved, a sudden blast of music hit the three of them.

'Sorry,' said John. 'I didn't realize the volume was up.' He turned the volume down.

Dawn apologized. 'I think it was my fault. I had quite a bit of loud music while you were in hospital. Like therapeutic.'

Will put his fingers to his lips. He wanted to listen. He frowned, as he always did when concentrating.

'Is that Monk?' he asked.

Nobody answered, because nobody really understood the question.

'It was a tune she liked,' said John, but he was answering a question nobody had asked.

THREE

Just A-Sitting and A-Rocking

Rachel worked at Glenn Travel in the centre of York. She could walk from the flat in ten minutes, or she could take a bus. In the rush hour, the bus took twenty minutes. She usually walked.

The travel agency was owned, run by and named after Joan Glenn. The name Glenn was the one item she had salvaged from a broken marriage. She had broken it herself, throwing out her husband a decade ago, citing several bookmakers and most of the nation's leading distilleries. She liked the name and it worked well over the door of the travel agency, with its overtones of moon landings and hints of transatlantic glamour. Her family name was Armitage and she argued that Armitage Travel would suggest an outfit specializing in cheap day returns to Barnsley and Doncaster.

Joan was in her late thirties, smoked too much, swore consistently, was a stone overweight and didn't give a damn. She and Rachel shared the work, whatever its volume. They had tried taking on temporary staff at busy times, but this always had the effect of making it rain, emptying the premises and silencing the telephone.

They spent much of their time on their telephones, sitting side by side behind a high counter.

'I have a copy of the booking form here in front of me, Mr Bradshaw,' said Joan, scowling at the receiver while she tried hard to smile with her voice. 'It says two seats facing the engine, non-smokers.' She ground out her cigarette in the already full ashtray, seeing in its mess the face of the betrayed Mr Bradshaw. 'And they gave you two smokers with their backs to the engine?'

She covered the mouthpiece with her hand, and

muttered at Rachel: 'I bet there was no paper in the sodding lavatory either.'

Rachel had little local difficulties of her own.

'Firenze *is* Florence, Mr Nicholson. Yes, the Italians have their own names for their own cities. Firenze, Roma, Napoli . . . that kind of thing.'

Minutes later, in their first coffee break of the day, they compared malicious notes about their customers.

'He's a right bloody pudendum, that Bradshaw,' said Joan, 'and I was right. There wasn't any paper in the lavatory. Silly bugger should have gone before he left home.'

'My Mr Nicholson didn't realize Firenze was the same as Florence, and when I explained he said: "Oh, do you mean like the Eurovision Song Contest?"'

'That's a bit out of left field. Pass the sugar.'

'We've both given up sugar.'

'Sod that.'

Rachel passed the sugar. Joan added two spoonfuls to her coffee.

'And how's bereavement treating you all?'

Rachel smiled at the question. She had often said Joan should be in the diplomatic corps. The result might be global destruction or eternal peace, but the decision would be made in five minutes, including the countdown.

'My Dad's only so-so. Dawn's terrific. Yes, we're OK.'

'No, you're not.'

Rachel shrugged. Joan continued:

'You're not. You can't fool me. There ain't no sanity clause.'

The older woman had the quality recommended by Hemingway: a built-in shit detector. Rachel knew it and she told the truth, as far as she could discern it:

'When somebody dies, you realize how little you really know about them. I want to know about my mother. I want to know what she was like when she was my age. But nobody'll tell me. My Dad can't, not at the moment anyway.'

'Your Mum's parents are still alive, aren't they?'

'Yes.'

'Parents know about kids. Fact of life. Even if they've screwed them up, they know about it.'

'I thought I might pop over to Grandma's at the weekend.'

'Go now.'

'I'm at work.'

'Finish your coffee and piss off.'

As Rachel was putting her coat on, she remembered: ' I said I'd meet Will from work. We're going to the pictures.'

'What to see?'

'Clint Eastwood, beating hell out of a few innocent bystanders.'

'Ring Will, tell him you've changed your mind. The odd bit of betrayal's very good for a man. Focusses the mind and body.'

Rachel hesitated, then reached for the telephone. It rang, as if in anticipation. She picked up the receiver.

'Hello, Glenn Travel.'

She listened briefly, then looked at Joan.

'It's your Mr Bradshaw. He's remembered something he forgot to complain about.'

'Shit,' said Joan.

The River Ouse at York is handsome, wide and occasionally too high; but most of the time it flows benignly and people sail boats upon it and use it as a pretty background for their holiday snaps.

The River Ouse at Selby, fourteen miles to the south, is narrower but tougher, a waterway that works for a living though not as hard as it once did. Here the river gathers strength before it arrives at Goole and spills into the mighty Humber – swollen and brown, but impressive enough to have been written about by Philip Larkin, and not many industrial rivers can say that.

Down by the riverside at Selby lived the Jacksons, Rachel's grandparents, in a neat, artisan terrace house of the sort romanticized by northerners in exile, and tarted up if they happen to have landed in Chelsea or Hampstead.

The Jackson house had landed happily in Selby, and was untouched by alien elements, apart from wind and weather. Grandpa Jackson, since his retirement from the railways, painted the house, inside and out, every two years. It sparkled, like its inhabitants, especially when Rachel came to call.

'Sit there,' ordered Mrs Jackson.

She nodded towards an inviting reproduction rocking-chair, a Christmas present from Rachel and Dawn two years previously. The grandparents had thanked them but resolutely refused to sit in it.

'It's like an open invitation to the undertaker to give you an estimate,' Mr Jackson had said.

The Jacksons loved their granddaughters, and they loved the chair, but it was kept strictly for visitors.

'I'll sit down when you've had your presents,' said Rachel.

She gave her grandfather two ounces of St Bruno, his favourite pipe tobacco.

'You shouldn't encourage him to smoke his pipe,' said Mrs Jackson, 'it's killing both of us.' She generally referred to it as St Michael, because it smelled as if he were smoking underpants.

Rachel dipped into her Habitat carrier and produced a six-pack of lager. As she handed these to her grandmother, Mr Jackson was nimble as ever with his counter-punch: 'You shouldn't encourage her to drink that stuff. It's poisoning her system and it makes her sing Doris Day songs.'

'Ignore him. Sit down.'

Rachel sat down. Her grandfather was about to do the same, in his much-loved armchair – 'It's never rocked in its life, but it fits the shape of my bum' – when his wife intervened.

'There's no point in you sitting down. You're going to make us a cup of tea.'

'Am I?'

Rachel volunteered.

'I'll do it.'

'You'll do nothing of the sort. We're emancipating ourselves. That's right, isn't it? It was in that book you lent me. The female whatdoyoucallit.'

'Eunuch.'

'What's a eunuch?' asked Mr Jackson.

'If you don't get that kettle on sharp, you'll find out soon enough,' said Mrs Jackson.

He decided to refuse the invitation and headed towards the kitchen. As he was filling the kettle, Mrs Jackson called to him: 'And when you've had your cup of tea, you can go to the allotment.'

'I don't want to go to the allotment.'

'Of course you do. You only think you don't.'

The marriage was a barrage of non-stop sparring that never came to blows, underpinned by a mutual dependence rarely acknowledged publicly, but shining like a beacon. Rachel warmed herself at its glow, but her adoration was tempered with an anger that so much native wisdom and curiosity should have been neglected by a society that had hurled them out of school in the 1930s, still unpolished and unfinished. It enraged her that her grandfather expressed gratitude for a working life spent on the railways, punctuated by a five-year gap defending democracy in the Western Desert and Italy.

'I've never been out of work,' he had said to her one day, when Mrs Jackson had sent both of them to the allotment because they were making too much noise.

'Society's given you far less than you're worth, Grandad. And you shouldn't be grateful.'

She was seventeen at the time and had just discovered a book of Karl Marx's edited highlights. He had smiled kindly on her indignation.

'That's your battle, sweetheart. We never fight our own battles. We fight them for our parents and for our grandparents. Whether they want us to or not. I daresay I have been cheated but I don't see it. I'm standing too close.'

'But would you like me to fight your battles, Grandad?'

'Yes please, love,' he had said, so quietly she could hardly hear him.

23

Today, after making the tea, he went to his allotment alone, first slipping his pipe and the St Bruno into his pocket. He had sensed women's talk in the air and, inevitably, talk about his daughter's death. He was not yet ready to be part of that.

When he had gone, the women poured themselves a second cup of tea. They too were not quite ready to talk about death.

'So did you enjoy *The Female Eunuch*?' said Rachel.

'She has some funny ideas about sex, does the lass. Couldn't stop laughing half the time. But yes, I like the principle of the thing. Me sitting here supping tea, and sending him off to the allotment. I like that. I like it a lot.'

Rachel protested: 'Female emancipation doesn't mean treating men badly.'

'I don't treat him badly. I just tell him what to do and he does it. But it's always things he wants to do in the first place. He loves going to his allotment. He never does any gardening when he's there. He just sits around smoking his pipe and yarning with his mates about the great days of steam engines. That's all right, isn't it? He can't talk to me about steam engines. Well he can, but I don't really listen.'

Rachel listened. It was a joy to pass books on to her grandmother – anything from *The Uses of Literacy* to *Catch-22* – and hear their themes yanked out, held up to the light and related directly to life as lived between the riverbank and the allotment. Mrs Jackson was a slow reader, but she got there in the end – even if her 'there' bore only a marginal relationship to the authors' assumed destinations.

Rachel attempted a summary of the discussion so far.

'So when you order him out of the house, and send him to the allotment, you're actually doing him a favour?'

'Of course I am. Have another biscuit.'

It was in part an invitation to herself, as she leaned forward and took another biscuit from the tray.

'And I'll tell you something else, our Ráchel. The day he dies, I chuck myself in the river.'

'Bet you don't.'

'You'll see, when the day comes. Any road, that's enough about death and dying. You said on the phone you wanted to talk about your Mam.'

Even after many years, Rachel constantly found herself wrongfooted by her grandmother. She would hedge about trivialities but always met the great universals head on.

'Isn't talking about Mum talking about death and dying?'

'We know about the death. It was a car crash. Nothing more to be said about that. We can talk about what she was like when she was alive. That's the only thing worth bothering about. Living.'

'Yes. That's what I want to talk about.'

'Talk about it.'

It emerged brusquely, like an order, and Rachel obeyed.

'Well, for one thing . . . did you know she was already pregnant when she married my Dad?'

'Good God, have you only just worked that out? Of course I knew. It's simple arithmetic, isn't it? And any road, I can spot a bun in the oven at a hundred yards. And what's the odds? You were born out of love, that's all that matters.'

'And did my Mum and Dad get married out of love or out of necessity?'

'There was no necessity. Your Dad could have walked away. That was made very clear. He chose not to. He's a good man, your father. Pure in spirit.'

In full flow, she paused, arrived at some private decision, then stood up and crossed to the sideboard. She opened a door, allowed a few items to tumble out on to the floor – a half-knitted pullover, her button box, Rachel's copy of *The Colour Purple* – then from the back corner pulled out a shoe box. She replaced the items that had fallen out in such a way that they were guaranteed to fall out again the next time she opened the door. It was a recurring memory from Rachel's childhood: her grandmother opening the door of the sideboard, and things falling out. The button box was special. She had learned to count using

25

Grandma's buttons, and the buttons had served as currency when her grandfather gave her instructions in pontoon, cribbage and the basic elements of gambling.

Mrs Jackson took the lid from the shoe box.

'This is all stuff about your mother.'

The box contained an unsorted mess of school magazines, speech-day programmes, holiday postcards, snapshots and oddments defying easy classification: two tickets stubs from a concert given by the Gerry Mulligan Quartet in the late 1950s, a bass string from a guitar, still in its wrapper, a photograph of a rugby player with an indecipherable autograph (the face was no longer familiar). Everything in the box had been filed under miscellaneous, but Mrs Jackson knew her way around it. She took out a paper wallet full of snapshots, spreading the photographs on the rug in front of the fire. She and Rachel knelt on the floor to look at them.

'These are when she first went to university.'

'Look at the scarf!'

'She told me you were really somebody if you had a long scarf so I knitted her one, all in the proper colours like. Your Grandad used to say she could be in Leeds before the end of the scarf had left home.'

The photographs were all in black and white. They showed eager young people smiling with the certainty that they could change the world and remake it in their own image. Bill Haley and the Comets had blown a wind of change and The Beatles were living in Liverpool, waiting to be invented. SuperMac was in office, Harold Wilson was lurking around the next corner but one, and it all seemed a century ago, in shades of grey.

Rachel looked for her mother in all the pictures. She saw a girl, dark-haired like herself, but different from the mother she had known in adult life. The woman she remembered was quiet and receptive – she would hear your confession and you need not be afraid; but the girl in the photographs was different. She was a ringleader. She seemed to be at the centre of all the groups, an initiator, a maker of mischief, the reckless heart of whatever matters were in hand.

'That's Rag Week,' said Mrs Jackson, pointing at a picture of a group of students, dressed with resolute abandon, perched on the back of a lorry. 'She's dressed up as a mermaid.'

'She doesn't look like a mermaid.'

'Maybe it was something else. Marilyn Monroe or General Eisenhower.'

'That must be Aldermaston.'

Her mother, wearing duffel-coat, trousers and scarf, was marching at the centre of the front rank of a procession, beneath a large CND banner. She was laughing. She believed the cause was just, and she believed it would be won. There was an edge of recklessness in that, too. At the time of her death her belief in the cause was no less passionate, but the hope was diminishing.

'Like mother, like daughter,' said Rachel, pointing at the badge in her lapel.

'Ban the generals. That's your best bet. Guns never hurt anybody. It's the silly sods that fire them.'

'Are there any photographs with her and my Dad?'

'I don't think so.'

'But didn't they meet at university?'

'Yes, but I don't think they took a photograph of it. It was a lecture about something or other. Probably the other.'

They both laughed.

'You're a very wicked woman, considering you're a grandmother.'

'I tried being good, but my system rejected it.'

As she spoke, she rummaged deeper in the shoebox and brought out a bundle of letters, tied around with string. Other, more sentimental people might have used pink ribbon, but Mrs Jackson believed in string.

'These might help you,' she said, handing the letters to Rachel, who started to untie them. 'Don't do that.'

'Why not?'

'Those are the letters your Mam wrote to us when she was a student. There's not many of them, but when she did write, they were long ones. Good letters. Proper sentences. Proper enough to fool us.'

'Why can't I read them now?'

'Take them home. Read them in your own time. If you start reading them now, I shall do the same, and I only stopped crying yesterday.'

Rachel took the letters and put them in the pocket of her coat, which was draped over the back of the rocking-chair.

'Look after them, and return them promptly.'

'I promise.'

Neither of them spoke, but a silent agreement was struck and Mrs Jackson started to pick up the photographs and put them back in the shoe-box. The two of them had touched enough nerves for the time being.

'Thank you,' said Rachel.

'You're very like your mother.'

'In what way?'

'She wouldn't take No for an answer.'

Mrs Jackson stood up, crossed to the sideboard, opened the door amd put the shoe-box back in its allotted place. The half-knitted pullover, the button box and the book fell on to the floor again. She replaced them, then shut the door quickly and firmly against them. She added, as the thought struck her: 'She wouldn't take Yes for an answer, either.'

It was late in the evening when Rachel left her grandparents to drive back to York. A detour of less than a mile would have taken her to her father's house, but she chose not to. She argued to herself that Will would be waiting for her. It was a rationalization.

She would have found a silent living-room. Dawn was doing homework, on the floor. John was listening to music, through a pair of headphones, but hearing other, more distant voices.

Dawn tidied her books and papers into a not very neat pile and stood up.

'I'm going to bed.'

He stared at her, then removed the headphones.

'I'm sorry, love?'

'I said I'm going to bed.'

'Good.'

He was part-way to replacing the headphones before feeling the twinge of paternal responsibility.

'Did you solve your homework?'

'Yes. I'll do the usual thing. Write the answers on my arm and cheat my way to an A minus.'

'Good.'

It was intended as a joke, but there was no sign that he had even registered her words, and laughter now lived in another country.

'Are you all right, Dad?'

'I'm nearly tired of people asking me if I'm all right,' he said, with a whisper of a smile.

'Me too. 'Cause we're not, are we?'

She needed to be out of the room. She needed to be in her own bedroom, with her little cast-off black-and-white TV set, and some late-night imported garbage. Even snooker would do.

'Good-night, Dad.'

She kissed him on his bald patch.

'Good-night, love.'

As she left the room, John retreated inside the music.

'He took the wrong ball there. He should have snookered him behind the green,' said Mr Jackson.

He was watching the snooker. Mrs Jackson was making her late-night check of the Births, Deaths and Marriages in the local paper, in case anyone she knew had undergone a vital change, undetected.

She glanced at the screen over the top of the newspaper, like a spy in a thriller.

'He's got nice hair, that one.'

'They all have nice hair. They have managers to make sure they have nice hair.'

'What about the bald ones? Isn't there a couple of bald ones?'

He ignored her. Snooker was much too important to be discussed in the language of hairdressers. He watched the well-groomed young player compile a fifty break, criticizing him ferociously but silently. The lad approached the game much too flashily, even if he was a millionaire at twenty-three.

'And what did our Rachel want?' he said, as a vital black wobbled in the jaws of the corner pocket, as happens to flashy young snooker players.

'You were here.'

'While I was at the allotment. What did you talk about then? I know when I'm being cleared out of the way.'

'She wanted to talk about Ann.'

'What did you tell her?'

'Enough.'

He started to clean out his pipe. She knew the procedure. She sometimes thought he took more pleasure from the gentle art of preparation than he did from smoking the damn thing. He often cleaned his pipe when they were on the edge of serious talk.

'Is that all you said? That sounds like a very short conversation.'

'I also told her I couldn't live without you.'

'Hellfire.'

'It's true, isn't it?'

He said nothing, but concentrated on scraping out the gunge from his pipe with his old penknife before tipping it into the remains of the fire.

'I see. You want time to think,' she said, sharply.

'It's true.'

She glanced across at the television as the well-groomed young lion playing a winning shot.

'That was well played.'

It was impossible to tell which game she was talking about.

* * *

Will had given up on the snooker game and gone to bed with the *Architectural Review*. He heard Rachel return, waited for her to come into the bedroom, but after ten minutes with no apparent attempt at communication he got up to investigate.

She was sitting at the living-room table, reading letters.

'I went to bed.'

She looked up from her reading.

'I thought so. The pyjamas are a vital clue.'

He walked across to the table and looked over her shoulder.

'Am I allowed to ask . . . ?'

'Letters my mother wrote to her parents when she was a student.'

'Are you going to read them all tonight?'

'There's not that many.'

'They seem fairly thick.'

She raised a hand, finding and clasping his.

'I have to read them, Will. I have to read them tonight.'

'Sure.'

'Why don't you go back to bed?'

'I think I'll go back to bed.'

She squeezed his hand, offering her face for a kiss and adding a sexy promise with her eyes.

'If you're still awake when I get there . . .'

He kissed her.

'I've got a hard day at the drawing-board tomorrow. Just give me a voucher. We'll redeem it at the weekend.'

After he had gone to bed, Rachel browsed through the letters. The handwriting was neat and well schooled but already suffering from the need to write quickly in examination rooms and also it seemed from impatience and excitement. The precision on page one of each letter rapidly gave way to a sprawling exuberance. They were letters written lovingly and frenetically. Sometimes her fountain-pen – a present for passing her A levels – had run dry, and a pencil or a smudgy ball-point had taken over.

The punctuation was occasional and approximate, but

the voice spoke clearly enough, at a distance of a quarter of a century.

Dear Family and Others Passing By

Forgive me my trespasses and long silences but we've been working hard on account of some rumour that's circulating about Finals and that puts the blocks on proper creative things like getting drunk and writing home to Dearly Beloved Ones including parents and dog.

A funny thing happened last night – I think I fell in love. It's all the fault of Jean-Paul Sartre who's a French existentialist and if you want to know what an existentialist is I'll send you some books under plain wrapper but I think you're probably an existentialist, Dad, so that must be a clue.

Any road, hoping to get a clue about whether you really are an Existlst, Dad, I went to this lecture on Jean-Paul S but also because it was free (I am broke again – any chance of a £?) I suppose if I come to think about it the lecture wasn't really free and was paid for by the State, i.e. the taxpayer, i.e. you, Dad – sorry, Dad – it wasn't free because you paid for it and all I did was to go to it and fall in love or something closely resembling ditto.

His name's John and he comes from Liverpool or perhaps Lancashire or Birmingham – one of those places – and afterwards we went for a drink because his Beloveds had just sent him some ££££s but not that many – he wasn't at the lecture on J-P S because he was broke but because he wanted to be there i.e. he's quite a serious sort of chap – not rich or handsome in fact there's a tiny hint of recession around the hairline though it curls nicely at the back and he's got sideboards which is probably a bit of a gesture in the face of eventual baldness but he listens – not many listeners in the world and as you know I need listeners . . .

Rachel turned the next page in the apparently endless wad. She was having difficulty in coming to terms with

32

her mother as chatterbox in search of a listener. It was not the woman she knew. Perhaps the birth of children transformed all women into listeners, if only on a temporary basis of twenty years or so.

She read on:

> I'll make him get his hair cut before I bring him home cos I know how you feel abt. long-haired intellectuals Dad and honestly if I could find a short-haired footballer I would and I have tried but they're all as thick as that word you said I shouldn't put in letters and they always want to show you their cartilages.
>
> I know I'm a bit daft where the opposite sex (pardon the expression) is concerned but bells are ringing in my ears and it isn't Christmas being as how it's June so this could well be the man I'm going to marry and I feel my Beloved Parents should be the first to know about it – am I reckless? If you want to impose restraint please write by return of post (if possible enclose a £) but if you think it's my business who I propose marriage to (that should be whom but I don't want to confuse you or me) then that's fine as well – I could use the £ either way.
>
> By the way did you know that they have done research in the Humanities Department here which is next door but one to the Union Bar which is naturally how I know about it and it (the research) proves that you two are the Greatest Parents in the world? By the time I write the next letter they'll have done research on Asia too and I'll let you know the results – your daughter would like you to know that she does love you madly as she also loves John from Liverpool or Lancashire or Birmingham.
>
> It might be Carlisle but wherever it is I am marooned in a romantic mist – your devoted and besotted and probably fairly stupid daughter Ann
> xxxxxxxx for Mum
> xxxxxxxx for Dad
> XXXXXXXXXXXXXXXXXXXXX for my bold mongrel Paddy

Rachel folded the pages and slipped them back into the faded envelope, which was addressed to 'The Wholly Fabulous Jacksons and their dog Paddy' and decorated with a carelessly drawn border of what looked like flowers.

She had heard family folklore about the dog; how he would whine at the front door five minutes before Mr Jackson was due home from work, and howl soulfully at the church bells every Sunday. Paddy had died soon after she was born, but survived as an occasional blur on snapshots and the subject of tales after Christmas dinner.

She wished she had known Paddy. He had obviously been a terrific dog. Even more, she wished she had known the young woman who had written the letters. They were possessed of an energy, a wildness and an echo of chimes at midnight that had no place in the mother she remembered. Rachel needed to hear the stories that would never be told at a family Christmas.

'My God! Couldn't you sleep?'

The sign on the door promised that Glenn Travel would open for business daily at 9.30 am, but it was unusual for both Joan and Rachel to be there on time. It was epoch-making for Joan to arrive five minutes early and find Rachel apparently hard at work, sitting at the computer keyboard, peering at the screen.

'Just doing a bit of personal overtime.' She looked up, and smiled, adding as an afterthought: 'Good morning, boss.'

'Jesus H. Tupperware! When did you last see your eyes? Talk about rissoles in the snow! Was it a good orgy? Did the bishop show up? Does he still do tricks with his mitre? I'll make some coffee. Where's the bloody spoon?'

All the questions were rhetorical, apart from the whereabouts of the spoon. Rachel ignored them all. The spoon always turned up eventually.

'I read late.'

'If you're going to go blind, reading late's a boring way to go about it.'

34

Joan disappeared into the back room, in search of the spoon. Rachel focussed on the keyboard and screen.

The computer was programmed to accept and record holiday bookings, calculate and codify the quarterly VAT returns, and resist Joan's attempts to kick it to destruction when it refused to speak her language. If talked to nicely, it could be persuaded to carry out simple arithmetic calculation.

'It's all numbers,' said Joan, looking over her shoulder while the kettle boiled.

'You're a woman of the world, aren't you?'

'More times than you've had hot dinners, sweetheart.'

'Give or take a week or two, it does take nine months to make a baby, doesn't it? It's more or less an accepted fact of life, wouldn't you say?'

'Unless you're an elephant or a whale.'

'This is strictly about the human species.'

'Allow nine months. That's my advice. It's what I told the bishop and the actress.'

'I'm not putting my name down.'

Rachel hit the 'Erase' button. The screen went blank.

'It's just that January minus June doesn't add up.'

'Of course it doesn't add up if it's minus. Have some coffee. Your brain needs a de-coke.'

Rachel started to open the morning mail. Joan, halted in mid-stream of some promising baby-talk, was in no mood for displays of efficiency.

'Come on, kid, give me the dirt. There's obviously something highly intimate and personal going on.'

'Maybe.'

'So aren't you going to tell me? I may not be your oldest friend but I'm certainly the crudest.'

'I'm sorry. It's highly intimate and personal.'

Joan shrugged. She realized Rachel was not joking.

'I respect your feelings, my dear. Take a week's notice.'

Rachel smiled. She knew her boss *was* joking.

She saved the highly intimate and personal talk for lunch-time with Will. Once a week they visited a local burger joint where they held competitions for the most inventive order. Will's entry today was: a jumbo quarter-pound Picasso-burger with post-Modernist french fries and a side order of cole slaw. He had brought a drawing with asterisks and subtitles. It was part of their tradition, but Rachel had forgotten to enter.

Will guessed the reason correctly.

'Is it because of the letters?'

'Yes.'

'Tell me about them. Properly.'

They had discussed the letters in bleary monosyllables between bathroom and breakfast, before agreeing to save the in-depth analysis for lunchtime. Rachel told her story, properly.

'The letters are . . . wonderful. She met Dad, fell in love with him at first sight at a lecture on Jean-Paul Sartre, and didn't even know whether he was from Liverpool, Birmingham or Carlisle.'

'Where is he from?'

'Somewhere near Norwich.'

'She was never that hot at geography, your mother. I was giving her directions to the flat, the first time she came to see it, and I realized she didn't actually understand the difference between North and South.'

'She had trouble with left and right as well.'

The waitress arrived with chili con carne. Despite the weekly Invent-The-Exotic-Burger-Of-Your-Dreams competition, they generally ordered the chili and took a chance on the consequences.

Rachel waited until the waitress moved away from the table, then said: 'The other thing I discovered was . . . my father isn't really my father.'

'That's a bit of a contradiction. It's like saying York Minster isn't really York Minster.'

'It's true, just the same.'

'Explain.'

'She met my Dad . . . the man I thought was my Dad . . . at a lecture on June 17th 1959. They got married in August. I was born on January 3rd 1960. I wasn't prema-

36

ture. I weighed nearly nine pounds and Mum told me I was about ten days late. I've checked the arithmetic. I was conceived two months before my parents met.'

'That's a clever trick.'

Will did a quick calculation on a serviette with his favourite felt-nibbed pen: the one he used for doodling Cubist burgers after the manner of Picasso.

'Does that make you a bastard? If it does, make sure you're a really mean one.'

'Not funny, Will.'

'No?'

She shook her head and looked out the window. The restaurant was in a narrow street, twin rows of elderly buildings overlooking a permanent traffic jam.

Rachel saw none of this.

'Legitimate, illegitimate, none of that matters a damn. What matters is somewhere out there in what we laughingly call the world . . . somewhere out there is my father. My real father. And I've never met him.'

'So?'

'I'd like to meet him. Say hello. Hi there, Dad. That sort of thing.'

'Does it matter? After all this time?'

'Half of him is me. So yes, it matters.'

'I'd like to ask you a really silly question.'

John was in the greenhouse, watering plants in a haphazard fashion, but content that vegetable life in general coped better with drowning than with thirst.

'You've been asking me silly questions as long as I can remember. One more won't make any difference.'

She hesitated. Physically he was almost fully recovered, and threatening go back to school the following Monday; behind the eyes the pain still prospered.

'Well? I'm waiting for the silly question.'

'When did you last see my father?'

'When I shaved this morning.'

It was good that he was joking again, and good that he was shaving regularly. Rachel had been alarmed by the symptoms of self-neglect and the prospect of lectures from her grandmother about people 'letting themselves go'.

'I've been doing my homework about the year 1959,' said Rachel, quietly and precisely. John was on his way to re-fill the watering-can from the tap in the yard. Instead, he put down the can, and gave all his attention to Rachel.

'I see.'

He sat down on an upturned wooden box.

'It's true. Your mother was pregnant when we first met. Only just. In fact she still had hopes that it might be a mistake. A trick of the light, she said. But it wasn't.'

'And you married her.'

'Oh yes. It was obvious. I loved her. I said: will you marry me? She said: does it matter that I'm pregnant? I said: it doesn't matter.'

'You're terrific.'

'I got myself a daughter called Rachel as a result. It was an offer I couldn't refuse.'

She leaned over, kissed him on his bald spot, then sat down on a box close by.

'Mum adored you, from the very first moment.'

'How do you know that?'

'She wrote to Grandma and said so. I've seen the letter. Love at first sight. In her own handwriting and signed with her name. That makes it evidence in law.'

'Well, yes, it *was* like that. Love at first sight, and second and third and on. It doesn't stay the same. It grows up. Matures. Less of a frenzy. More certain. It gets better and richer. I know it because I've lived through it. I know it in my bones, daughter.'

He occasionally called her 'daughter' in a gently tongue-in-cheek manner, distantly modelled on Old Mother Riley addressing her daughter Kitty, but now absorbed into the family custom and practice. His use of the word always indicated he was very serious indeed.

'You still haven't answered my silly question.'

'I don't know the answer to your silly question. Ann told me she was pregnant. She said she'd rather not tell

38

me who the man was. I respected that. I never asked her that. She never told me.'

'No theories?'

'None at all.'

They sat quietly. He started to nibble at a finger-nail, then stopped himself when he caught her glance.

'I need a hug,' he said.

'Me too.'

They embraced then, as they broke away, he asked: 'Am I allowed a silly question?'

'Sure.'

'Even if I'm not your father, may I still be allowed to call you daughter?'

'Don't be silly. Look . . . even if I find out who he was, and then if I find him, and he turns out to be a triple Nobel prize-winner, or lead singer with the Amadeus String Quartet, or just a two-bit punk pushing dope on street corners . . . whatever *he* is, *you*'ll always be my Dad. That's permanent. That's in my bones, father.'

She was never more in earnest than when she called him 'father', but he was still disturbed.

'You said . . . if you find him. Does that mean you're going to look for him?'

'Oh, I don't know.'

She was deliberately offhand. It fooled neither of them.

Her grandmother was not helpful.

'I am a bad girl. I borrow letters from my Grandma, and I do the sums, and I know it takes nine months to make a baby. So . . . when did you last see my father?'

'Last Thursday.'

'My real father.'

'Your real father's the one who brought you up for the last twenty-six years.'

Mrs Jackson's mouth was set solid. Rachel had seen the same expression on her face when carpetbaggers came to the door selling cheapskate religion or the Conservative Party. She had also seen the expression on her own face, in the mirror, two or three times a week since the age of five.

'Somewhere I have a biological father. When Mum got pregnant she must have told you who he was.'

'I'm saying nothing.'

'I have a right to know.'

'I'll grant you that, but I'm still saying nothing.'

Both mouths were set solid. Rachel stood up, zipped up her anorak and crossed to the door.

'Is my Grandad at the allotment?'

'Either there or at his club.'

'I'll go and ask him.'

'He won't say anything. He wouldn't dare.'

'That's for him to decide. Men can be liberated as well, you know . . .'

Mrs Jackson shouted at her as she opened the door.

'Rachel! We *promised*!'

'Promised.'

She repeated the word, not questioning her grand-mother's statement, but seemingly testing its strength.

'She made us promise. Me and your Grandad. When she met John and decided that's who she was going to marry. She said to us . . . promise you'll never tell anybody who it was.'

'I'm not anybody. I'm the child. It's my father we're talking about.'

'A promise is a promise.'

Rachel unzipped her anorak and walked back to the rocking-chair. She sat down.

'I shall find out.'

'Maybe you will. Maybe you won't. But I shall never tell you.'

The chair squeaked on its rockers.

'And I'll tell you something else,' said Rachel. 'I shall know him when I see him. If I walk into a room and he's there, I won't need any introductions. I shall know him. I promise you that.'

'I must get your Grandad to take his oilcan to that chair.'

* * *

After the evening meal was the best part of the day. It carried no obligations or responsibilities for Rachel and Will. They listened to music, completed one-third of the *Guardian*'s grown-up crossword, discussed and resolved a few cosmic dilemmas, drank freshly-ground coffee, played Scrabble or Trivial Pursuit, moaned about the lousy American programmes on television, made erotic and fanciful plans for bedtime; the permutations were infinite and often Will did drawings to match. It was the one period in the day when time was not of the essence. There were no appointments to keep and nobody was phoning back in five minutes.

Unexpected visitors were always made welcome but they dented the peace and sanctity of the evening. The doorbell rang as they were listening to Delius and pondering alternative energy sources for when the oil ran out.

'Damn!' said Will, who was on the brink of a great thought.

'It's probably my long-lost father.'

'If's he wearing a red carnaton and carrying a copy of *The Times*, I'll let him in. If not . . .'

Rachel looked at the shambles on the dining table and around the fireplace area while Will answered the door. She decided to leave everything. Only a close friend or a total stranger would call at ten in the evening. A close friend wouldn't mind and a total stranger wouldn't matter.

Will returned with Dawn, wearing her beloved hundred-year-old duffel-coat and carrying a Greenpeace shopping bag.

'It's your little sister,' he said.

'What are you doing here? You should be hard at work preparing to fail your A levels.'

'I've been on the town with a few comrades.'

She pronounced it with a short 'a' – the Russian way, filtered through a Yorkshire sieve.

'I thought I might score for some pudding and coffee.'

'There's coffee,' said Will, 'but no pudding. We can offer you an apple.'

'Don't like apples. They're good for you.'

Will poured her some coffee. She sat down beside Rachel on the settee, in what she knew to be Will's place.

'Is it a social call?' Rachel asked.

'Sort of. It's always nice to see my common-law brother-in-law. And my half-sister.'

She smiled with her best charm as Will gave her coffee, in a souvenir mug from Skegness, a place nobody even in the extended family could remember visiting.

'What's with the half-sister?' said Rachel. 'Have you been listening at keyholes again?'

'I've got the greenhouse bugged. You really are a shit-stirrer, aren't you?'

'Wash your mouth out with soap and water this instant!' said Will, knowing he would be ignored.

'I came here to help you and that's my reward! Abuse and derision. Not to mention no pudding.'

'What do you mean? You've come to help?'

Rachel knew her sister was serious, despite the surface trappings.

'You want to find your long-lost father? I've brought you a valuable clue.'

She delved into the Greenpeace bag and produced an LP record. Will took it from her and started to read the sleeve notes. He was an obsessive reader of sleeve notes and claimed they were a better education than the average university.

'Are his fingerprints on this?'

'I'm going off you, Will, you really are a bit thick at times.'

'Tell me,' said Rachel.

'Right. Well, you know Dad's been depressed since Mum died. Obviously. So have I but I'm immensely brave.'

'True,' said Will, kissing her on top of her head before sitting down on the arm of the settee.

'So night after night he sits on his own while I'm pretending to do homework, and over and over again he plays this tune. He played it when you were round the night he came out of hospital.'

'It's a Thelonious Monk tune,' said Will. 'He told us it was a tune your mother liked.'

'I asked him about that. He said yes, it was one of Mum's favourites, but she *never* played it because it reminded her of somebody. Got that? Reminded her of somebody. I'll give you three guesses. And it's a hundred-to-one on the right guess is your long-lost Daddy.'

'That's the clue?' said Rachel.

'My best offer.'

'And what is it called?'

' "Misterioso".'

FOUR

Doggin' Around

Fantasy had always come easily to Rachel.

As a very little girl, she had wanted to be Her Majesty The Queen when she grew up. When she discovered the title was not vacant, other possibilities began to haunt her imagination: Judy Garland, Bambi, any one of The Beatles' girlfriends, Ann Jones, Miss Piggy, Lucinda Prior-Palmer and Mrs Hodges, the PE teacher. In her late teens, the onset of political fervour and a semblance of maturity produced a new set of role models: Sylvia Pankhurst, Emma Goldman, Pat Arrowsmith and Nina Simone.

Once upon a happy time in bed, Will had summarized her fantasy life with his customary gentle astringency: 'You really want to be a Greenham woman with an electric blanket and a voice like Ella Fitzgerald's.'

The fantasy of private detection was new and she had to work at it. The Los Angeles school of private eye she found a little heavy on the machismo, though she was prepared to walk down a mean street with the best of them. The Christie school of country-house homicide left her lukewarm. Most of the characters were so unappetizing she would happily put the cyanide on draught and dispose of the entire cast with maximum speed and efficiency. On greater reflection she realized that the Christie world-view, and especially its sour assessment of the English middle class, was a vision she felt comfortable with.

Splicing these elements, her detective role crystallized. She became Philip Marple.

It was one thing to have a fantasy; it was quite another to apply it to real life, without an instruction kit. The quest was simple to define. She had to find her father; but how should Philip Marple set about the job? She had a vague idea she should be charging herself fifty dollars a

44

day plus expenses, but beyond that the only practical course of action she could think of was to buy a notebook. She bought a notebook.

One afternoon when Joan was out at a long lunchtime promotional piss-up, Rachel opened the notebook, and stared at the first blank page.

She numbered the page. She called it 1. That was easy. Then she pondered a main heading. In her mind it was a quest, but that carried overtones of holy grails and promised lands, all a bit excessive when the quest was for nothing more than a man. He might be her father, but she didn't expect anyone superhuman. A bloke was a bloke was a bloke.

She wrote the word PROJECT, and underlined it. It felt practical and professional. It was borrowed from Will. Architects spent all their lives working on projects. It might be demolishing and rebuilding another city or it might be a bathroom extension for the people next door. Either way, it was still a project.

It looked very good on the page: PROJECT.

Fifteen minutes later, after a telephone conversation about a WI trip to the bulb fields in Holland, she wrote another word on page 1. The word was *Witnesses*. Beneath it she listed the people who were around at the time of her conception, with appropriate comments. She looked at what she had written:

Page 1
PROJECT
My father.
Witnesses
Grandparents – won't talk – sworn to silence.
Dad – doesn't know – probably unfit to plead.

She was pleased with her work. It was neat, concise and accurate. It was also, for all practical purposes, useless. She tried another heading: *Alternative Information Sources*. It felt good, and had a modern radical tang. She pondered: what the hell did it actually mean? Easy: it meant who else would know the people around her mother during her time at University. Beneath the heading she wrote: *University Authorities*.

Before she could list any more alternative information sources, Joan returned, brimming over with Blue Nun and horror stories about the tourist trade. Rachel closed the book and slipped it in her bag. Philip Marple crawled back into her head, and re-emerged at the flat, late in the evening.

Will had set up his drawing-board on the dining table, and was catching up with a project for an Old People's Home. He was beginning to lose patience with the logistics of a closed geriatric community.

'I've provided so much wheelchair access, there's hardly any room to walk.'

He expected her to attack him for being ageist or disablist or maybe even walkist, but there was no sign that she had heard him. She was lying full-length on the rug in what she sometimes called her Elinor Glyn mode, but sin was not high on her immediate agenda. She was amending her Project notes made earlier in the day. 'My father,' she had decided, sounded too grandiose as an object of the investigation – as if she were searching for God. She deleted the 'My'. 'Father' was a totally acceptable definition, and would avoid confusion with the man she would always know as Dad.

Will tried again. He cherished their silences, when each of them was involved in a separate, small, but never secret, adventure: reading a book, doing the *Guardian* Quick Crossword slowly, searching for a missing pound in a bank statement; but he needed a tiny spurt of conversation at intervals. It was like that when they were out together. They rarely walked arm-in-arm or otherwise enmeshed, but they always held hands when crossing roads, or climbing stairs, or when the pavement was icy. He was sure and certain in their friendship but needed to warm his hands on it periodically.

'I just said something really witty.'

'Ha ha,' said Rachel.

'Thank you. Now shall I tell you what I said?'

'You said you'd provided so much wheelchair access,

46

there wouldn't be any room to walk. And yes, I think it's really witty. That's why I laughed. Eventually.'

'Isn't it ageist? Or disablist?'

'No. Just architectist.'

They traded smiles across the room. Comforted by the exchange, Will returned to his drawing. He was battling with one of architecture's universal dilemmas. If he put the lavatories in the best place for the people, they were in the worst place for an efficient and economic drainage layout. The converse was also true. That was what made it a dilemma. It puzzled and annoyed him that earnest books about Frank Lloyd Wright, Mies van der Rohe and Le Corbusier somehow never mentioned this. He was aware of the Post-Modernist-Hi-Tech approach – or whatever the smartarses were calling it this week – whereby you wrapped all the plumbing in stainless steel and strung it around the building like Christmas decorations, but once he started brooding along these lines, it was a sure sign he was tired.

He was on the edge of a great discovery – that if he changed the plan of the building into a mirror image of itself – a kind of left-handed version of his original conception – the people's lavatories *and* the drains might find unity, harmony and delight, when Rachel dragged his thoughts into a totally different galaxy.

'If I write to the registrar of the university,' she said, 'do you think they'd send me a list of students?'

'If you want a list of students, I'm sure that's the right way to go about it. Which university? What list? Like what, with love and respect, the hell are you talking about?'

'My father.'

'Your father, as opposed to your Dad?'

'Yes.'

They had clarified the difference during the last conversational break but one. Now Will tried to clarify Rachel's logic.

'The idea being that if you have a list of students who were contemporary with her, you can check them all out, one by one, until you find your father?'

'Something like that.'

'Do you realize how many students you're talking about?'

'One.'

'We don't know whether he was in the same department as your Mum. We don't know whether he was in the same year. We're talking about any student who was at university during the three years that she was there. That's probably five thousand people at least.'

'Divided by two. Half of them would be women and I know my father wasn't a woman.'

'So.'

'What would I do without your logical mind to wreck all my best wheezes?'

'We'd be swamped with lists of students, that's what.'

She closed the notebook, stood up and wandered to the drawing board. She stood behind him and put her arms around his neck. He enjoyed that. It was like wearing a warm, pliable and sometimes naughty muffler. This time the pressure was a plea for help.

'What do I do, Will?'

'You need a mole. A grass. A snout. Track down some of her old student mates.'

'Exactly. Back to the registrar.'

'Bollocks.'

'What have you got against the registrar?'

'Nothing. I'm sure he's a lovely guy. Fond of animals., Gives his old suits to War on Want. He might even be a Mahler freak. But that doesn't help you. It's far too complicated.'

'All right. Tell me something that isn't complicated.'

'Christmas-card lists.'

'Huh?'

'Your Mum was a methodical woman. I bet she had a Christmas-card list. You might even find last year's Christmas cards kicking around. Look for the ones with messages scribbled on the inside cover. You know the sort of thing. An apology for not writing a proper letter and a list of the kids' GCE passes.'

48

She squeezed her arms a little more tightly around his neck.

'You're a very wonderful human being. Can I do anything for you?'

'You could go easy on the strangulation. Help me through the valley of the shadow of lavatories. Make some coffee.'

'I can score two out of three,' she said, on her way to the kitchen to fill the kettle.

In bed she lay awake for nearly an hour, remembering. It was another of Will's ideas. Dredge in the memory for her mother's voice, talking about student days.

Trouble was she could remember next to nothing. Was it that men were more prone to that brand of nostalgia than women – those all-lads-together yarns that started with seventeen pints and ended with arbitrary thefts from BR? Or was it that parents' stories were always tedious to their children? Rachel could recall being angry when her mother was less than frantic to hear every last detail of a school hockey match. That was against the rules. The rules said parents needed to know the fine grain of the next generation's existence – every mark dropped in a Maths test, every emotional quiver at the school disco, every friendship confirmed, every betrayal underlined. Children were reporters. Parents were listeners. That was the arrangement.

Now, when Rachel needed to remember, she couldn't. She couldn't even remember *why* she couldn't remember. Was it because her mother had never talked about her student days? Or was it because she talked about them and nobody in the family ever listened?

Rachel realized: we never listen when we should, and when we need to listen, it's generally too late.

She tried to sleep. It usually came easily to both of them. Sometimes Will would say 'Race you to sleep' as they switched off their bedside lights, and next day nobody could remember who won.

Names floated into her mind . . . Sarah and Helen,

49

Gillian and Margaret . . . women's names, all of them. But was it her mother's voice speaking them, or was it her own, or was it some other voice from another dream? Outside in the street, a cat was crying for love and someone was failing to start a car. It was depressingly like the home life of Philip Marple.

Next day she took a long lunch-hour, by agreement.

'I owe you at least three,' said Joan, 'but try not to get as pissed as I do.'

'Pissed doesn't come into it.'

'Sex?'

'No.'

'You might as well work.'

Rachel drove to the family home. John was back at school and Dawn, after a period when she had rejected canteen food, had resumed battle with the school-meals service. She was researching a *Which?*-type survey which she planned to present to the Education Committee, with medical reports and the odd post mortem.

Rachel let herself into the house and went upstairs to what had been her parents' bedroom. In a dressing-table drawer she found her mother's address-book and, confirming Will's instinct, about a dozen of last year's Christmas cards. The family usually received about a hundred cards, so these must be from special people.

Again as Will had predicted, there were messages in most of them.

'We *must* get together soonest. Stacks of evil gossip about mutual friends piling up in my head. Whatever became of you know who? Solidarity, as always, Helen and Co.'

It sounded promising. Helen was one of the names echoing in her mind overnight. She checked the address-book. Under the letter H the name Helen was listed, with a local telephone number. There was no surname.

She dialled the number and heard the ringing tone, realizing she had not planned an opening to what could be an awkward and confused conversation. Will's advice, in all situations, was to trust the instinct. He generally cited Mahler as evidence. The ringing continued. Rachel decided to give it ten more rings. On her silent count of seven the receiver was picked up at the other end.

'Hello.'

A woman's voice, clear but uncertain.

'I wonder, could I speak to Helen, please?'

'Speaking, more or less.'

'This is Rachel. Ann's daughter. Ann who died.'

Helen's uncertainty filtered down the line. Rachel felt she was walking on slippery ground, without knowing why; but at least Helen identified her.

'Ann who died. Yes, got it. Saw you at the funeral. You're very pretty. Mind how you go. There are vultures out there.'

Rachel tried her brisk travel-agency manner, as if confirming a package tour of selected Greek Islands.

'I'd very much like to come and talk to you. About my mother. There are a few things about her student days that . . .'

Helen interrupted, the voice suddenly decisive.

'Come now.'

'Now?'

'I don't exactly get swamped with people wanting to come round to see me. Definitely not swamped. Oh yes. A giant step for mankind. Come now. I'll put some gin on a low light.'

Helen lived in a detached bungalow about a mile away, near enough on Rachel's way back into the city. It looked as if it had been built from a remaindered copy of the *Daily Mail Book of House Plans* with a few pages missing. Bay windows, leaded lights, stucco and artificial stone clamoured and competed for attention. Somewhere a front door was hiding.

Fortunately Helen was standing in the doorway, waiting for Rachel as she parked the car in a pebbled drive almost big enough to park a car. She was a trim woman, wearing a green trouser suit, and looked in good shape at a range of twenty feet. Close to, the lines and sinews told a

51

different story with small prospect of a happy ending.

'Come on in, dear,' she said, with a firm hand-clasp and, not surprisingly, a fleeting odour of warm gin. 'Come into the living-room.'

Rachel had lived with an architect long enough to know what to expect: in estate-agent's language, a spacious and desirable through lounge. In reality, the space was mean, the proportions ugly and it was the last place to satisfy any normal person's desires. It was also a prime example of a middle-class slum. Every surface was dusty, all the colours muted. It was like walking into an old-fashioned sepia photograph with a matt finish. Helen read her visitor's reaction. No doubt she read that reaction with each occasional visitor and she had her speech at the ready.

'It's a bit of a tip, but I'm a single-parent family with no kids. Only me and the cats.'

There were no cats to be seen, but their lifestyle hung on the air. Rachel looked at her watch at the same moment that she sat down. It was not a chair she wanted to sit on for too long. It felt contagious.

'I won't be able to stay long, I've already used up my lunch-hour . . .'

'Drink?'

'No thank you.'

'You don't mind if I sip quietly while we talk? It helps me concentrate. When I'm fully concentrated I'm half my normal size, but retain all my natural juices.'

It was a practised line, but a sparky one. There was a lively woman trapped inside this bungalow and God knows what else. She clung tightly to a tumbler of what could have been good clean water on the rocks, according to the visual evidence.

'Am I right . . . you were with my mother at university?'

'The legendary class of '59. I'll drink to that.'

She did. It was rather more than a sip. Rachel sensed that Helen might know all the answers she was seeking, but she would have to be swift with the questions, before

52

the drink took effect. Nose in the tramlines, she headed straight for the depot.

'Nineteen fifty-nine. That's the year I was conceived.'

'Oh yes, dear. I've known you since you were an embryo. And a scandal on the campus.'

Helen had trouble with the phrase, but took pains, and it emerged more or less intact, its meaning clear.

'Was I a scandal on the campus?'

'What? A scandal? You bet. Shock-horror. Take out the front page. What a shambles. Happy days.'

She drank to her memory of happy days. Rachel sensed that straight talk was probably the best policy.

'And who was the father of the embryo?'

'Your beloved Daddy?'

'Yes.'

'Haven't a clue.'

'Did she swear you to secrecy?'

Helen laughed. It was a rasping sound, short on gaiety. 'Nobody would ever swear me to secrecy. Waste of time, my lovely. Once I get started on the healing fluids . . .' she held up the now almost-empty glass as Exhibit A, '. . . there is no way I can recognize a secret when I see one. Indiscretion, thy name is Helen. I've never been asked to launch a ship. That's a shame. I should sue somebody.'

Her mind had slipped into the veering mode. Like a careless piano player, she had lost her place in the music. Rachel persisted.

'But can you remember the names of any of the men who were around at the time?'

'Sure. There were lots. Any name you care to name. Tom, Dick, Harry, Peter and Paul, Matthew, Mark, Luke and John. Not forgetting the Acts of the Apostles. They were very sweet. What became of sweetness? I used to have some. It looked so nice in the shop window, but when I got it home and unwrapped it . . .'

The words ran into a silence and she stood up. Her glass was empty.

'Are you sure you won't join me in a little drop of medicinal purposes?'

'I'm driving.'

'A good girl. What became of good girls?'

She wandered out of the room, returning quickly with a replenished glass. Rachel wondered, in the irrational mood of the occasion, whether the gin really was on a low light in the kitchen.

'Can you remember anyone . . . any man . . . who was a special friend of my mother's?'

'Not really. Everybody went around with everybody else. Whenever the music stopped we changed partners. Excluding sex. Sex hadn't been properly invented. We talked about it a lot. Your mother did it. That was unusual. Mostly we smoked cigarettes instead. That's probably highly significant.'

The haunting notes of 'Misterioso' drifted across Rachel's mind.

'The man . . . the father of my embryo . . . I think he was probably interested in jazz. Does that help?'

'Nothing helps.'

Helen stared into her glass, looking for help. The sun was shining in from the bay window behind her. Back-lit, it was difficult to tell if she was crying. It was possible.

Then, abruptly, she stood up and walked across the room to an old-fashioned record-player, with built-in speaker, four speeds and an auto-change device. It stood on the floor. Beside it a plastic record rack, designed to hold twenty LPs, crouched under the burden of twice that many, wedged in at odd angles.

'Music,' said Helen, pulling out a record and dislodging each of its neighbours so they slid on to the floor. She left them there to gather more moss. The record in her hand was Frank Sinatra's 'Songs for Swinging Lovers'.

'Reminds me of the class of '59,' she said, sliding the record from the sleeve, and dropping it on to the turntable, too hard for the long-term fidelity of its microgrooves. She pressed the 'Start' lever. Nothing happened.

'Broken. Every damn thing's broken.'

'I think it needs plugging in,' said Rachel, who could see the power lead trailing free.

Helen lost interest in the music, and its power sources. She turned, looked at Rachel.

'I'll tell you my secret about 1959. Promise not to tell anybody.'

'I promise.'

'1959 is the last time I remember being happy.'

As Rachel walked down the path towards her car, she could hear Sinatra's knowing voice, faintly husky and inch-perfect, coming from the bungalow. The song was 'You Make Me Feel So Young'. Combined with warm gin, it seemed like a deadly combination.

'Good God! You went to see old Helen? Has she tried to top herself lately?'

'I didn't ask,' said Rachel. She was beginning to dislike Brian. His was another name common to her mother's Christmas cards and address-book. When she rang him, he had been very warm and welcoming.

'Let me give you lunch. I love talking about old times and, sure as hell, my kids never want to listen.'

It was a friendly start, followed by early warning signals.

'Besides, it's good for my reputation to be seen dining with a pretty girl. Your big chance. Make a happy man feel very, very old.'

'How do you know I'm pretty?'

'Forgive me if it's a sensitive area, but I saw you at the funeral.'

Meeting Brian, face to face, across a corner table of a resolutely unpretentious bistro almost in the shadow of the Minster, she found his warmth was blended with slickness, and he had a haircut to match. Clearly there were bald patches lurking beneath it, at temple and crown, but they were concealed with a complicated and expensive system of whorls, like a giant thumbprint. The edifice was heavily lacquered against possible embarrassment from high winds off the plain of York. Try to run your fingers through that lot, she thought, and it would rattle.

Over starters, he had given her a quick CV of his postgraduate years.

'Lousy degree in Modern Languages. Didn't want to teach. People weren't queueing up to talk to me in French or Spanish, so I took my accountancy exams. Had some thoughts of travelling the world, selling tractors or toilet rolls. Ended up dabbling in property. Estate agent. Insurance. I'm a middleman. Tell me what you want, I'll get it for you. It'll cost you ten per cent of the gross.'

'I want to know the name of my father.'

She had decided there was a plain-speaking Yorkshireman lurking beneath the hairdo, and it might not be too late to find him.

'How much do you know?'

'I know John isn't my father. My mother was already pregnant when they met. Therefore somebody else is my father. I need to know where fifty per cent of my genes came from.'

'What did Helen tell you?'

'I think she had great trouble remembering what happened yesterday. 1959 is pushing it a bit. Though she says she was happy then.'

Brian was a smoker between courses. He offered Rachel a cigarette. She shook her head. He lit one for himself, without asking her permission. She relegated him to the Fourth Division. He drew deeply on the cigarette, and narrowed his eyes against the smoke. He had pulled on a sincere face, as if donning a balaclava. Confession hung over the table along with the smoke.

'If I'd had my way, I would have been your father.'

'Meaning?'

'I tried to get your mother into bed with me and she said No.'

'She said Yes to somebody.'

'That's what hurt. She said Yes to somebody else.'

And she said No to you, thought Rachel: good old Mum.

'So, accepting that a woman has a right to discriminate in her choice of sexual partner, have you any idea who it might have been? This man she found marginally more acceptable than you?'

56

He did not respond to her irony. She guessed it was a commodity of no interest to him, since you couldn't cream ten percent off the top.

'There was a great conspiracy of silence when your Mum got pregnant. I tried to find out who the father was. I asked everybody. I even asked her. I wanted to know, for obvious reasons.'

'You must have had some theories.'

'There were a few guys in the hunt at the time in question. I wouldn't like to point a finger at any one in particular. I could rattle off names, if you like, but God knows where they are now. In prison probably. They were all pretty crazy. Assorted drunks and perverts.'

I bet they were all pretty ordinary, Rachel decided: late adolescent, spotty and scared, puking in the Gents after three pints of draught bitter and calling it maturity.

'In any case, I think you're going about it the wrong way, sweetheart.'

'Sweetheart' felt like a negotiating ploy.

'Tell me the right way.'

'Talk to the best friend. Whenever a girl gets into trouble, she's bound to tell her best friend. It's elementary psychology. Yes, that's your best bet. Find the best friend.'

'That's perfect. Except I don't know the best friend.'

'Oh God, all I can remember is her name was Sarah. Can't remember her other name, but it's probably changed anyway.'

Rachel nodded. She had found the name Sarah among the Christmas cards and telephone numbers and had transferred it to her private detective's notebook. Indeed, Sarah was next on her list of contacts – a listing based on geography. She had started with Helen and Brian because they were closest to home. As a result she had met a dipsomaniac – maybe not clinically but certainly a dedicated amateur – and now a decaying Lothario.

Brian called for the bill with a discreet sign to the waiter, then paid it with a gilded credit card that bestrode all other credit cards like a colossus. The waiter, who was new, had never seen such a card, and took it away to check its pedigree with a proper grown-up waiter.

As they waited, Brian lit another cigarette. Rachel had counted seven during the meal.

'This has been great fun,' he said. 'Maybe we can do it again some time?'

He raised one eyebrow, or maybe lowered the other, a quizzical gesture intended to pass for charm. It was probably past its best in 1959, and it worked no better on the daughter than it had on the mother.

'Why?' said Rachel.

'Because this has been fun. We could have some more fun.'

'I'm very grateful for the time you've given me, and for the help, and for the lunch. But I live with a nice man called Will, and we have a television set, a video, a stereo unit, a bed and we both go to the public library once a week. That's as much fun as I can cope with.'

He shrugged. The shrug looked as if it had been used many times before, at least as often as the eyebrow tilt.

'You're a very attractive woman. You can't blame me for trying.'

She did blame him for trying, but didn't bother saying so.

Sarah McLaren was head of a large school on the outskirts of Leeds, Bradford or Huddersfield, depending on the direction of approach, and individual patriotism. Rachel arranged to see her the week after her brief encounter with Brian. The demands of private detection had made too many inroads into her working week at Glenn Travel and she waited until her next half-day. It seemed the decent thing to do.

The school was healthily noisy, decently untidy and gave off a sense of order and fun. Sarah radiated the same qualities. Rachel assumed there was a connection. It was a relief to find someone of her mother's generation who had reached her late forties with an apparently firm grip on commonsense and sensibility. She said as much, and felt safe in doing so.

58

'Don't get me wrong, but it's marvellous to meet one of Mum's crowd who's still in one piece. Nothing personal, but you do seem to be all in one piece.'

'Compared with whom?'

Rachel told her. Sarah laughed, not because she thought Helen or Brian were very funny, but because laughter was in her opinion one of the few constructive responses to the human condition.

'You picked a right pair of jokers there. Brian lives with the sad truth that he didn't actually invent sexual intercourse. If he had, he could have claimed a royalty on every screw from here to eternity. He's like a stamp-collector. He won't realize it isn't humanly possible to get the set.'

'What about Helen?'

'Chose the wrong parents. Daddy was a frigging brigadier, like the song says. Travelled the world trying to find bits of the British Empire to protect. Helen went to a string of lousy boarding schools, came to the conclusion her parents didn't give a sod about her. Ended up not giving a sod about herself. It's the obvious conclusion, if you think about it.'

'But you're all right?'

'Me? I'm amazingly ordinary and content. Married a good man, got two handsome kids, and I run a good school. Don't believe all that crap in the papers about comprehensive schools being full of protection racketeers and hoodlums. We're only half full. Besides, the kids need to learn how to be O level gangsters in case they end up in the City of London. What's so funny?'

Rachel was smiling. It followed that Sarah wanted to know why. This was a woman who zoomed through her days asking why.

'I'm smiling because you make me laugh. I'm also smiling because I recognize you.'

'Of course you do. I was at the funeral.'

'From Mum's photographs. I was looking at some old snapshots from university days. I didn't recognize Helen or Brian when I looked at them again, but you're on all of them, and you haven't changed.'

'Bollocks. I've got wrinkles, stretch marks, grey hairs, an overdraft, and I droop in places where once upon a time I didn't even have places. I'll tell you something. All tits should have "Gravity wins in the end" stamped on them. I'm going to write to the manufacturers about it.'

A bell rang somewhere in the school. It was followed by the ferocious clatter of feet as education regrouped for the next slice of the syllabus. Sarah enjoyed talking but the bell reminded her there was an agenda to get on with.

'What did you want to talk about? As if I didn't know . . .'

'I want to know the identity of my father.'

Sarah nodded. She knew all the time.

'No bullshit, Rachel.'

It was a relief to be called by her name, instead of being patronized by unlicensed endearments.

'No bullshit, Sarah.'

'Your mother and I were best friends. At the age of nineteen that has special significance. You're never as close to your friends as you are in late adolescence. Negative reasons. The world's big and frightening so you huddle together for warmth. No matter. We were best friends and I made a promise.'

'You promised you wouldn't tell anybody the name of the man?'

'I did. And at the time I made the promise I was closer to Ann than I've ever been to any other human being, including my husband, whom I love dearly. Can you give me any good reasons why I should break my promise?'

'I'm that man's daughter. He's my father. I don't think you have a moral right to keep the information from me.'

Sarah was no longer smiling. She was in a tiny room in a students' hostel, over a quarter of a century ago, hearing a confession, a cry for help and a plea for silence.

'This might hurt you, but I don't think you were a child of love.'

'As long as it wasn't rape.'

'Certainly not rape. A mixture of lust, draught bitter and sheer bloody daftness.'

60

'I can think of worse ways of starting a life.'

Sarah doodled on a notepad. Though the desk was layered in books, timetables, forms and indefinable pieces of paper, it was the only doodle in sight.

'Besides,' said Rachel, persisting, 'I know his favourite tune. It's called "Misterioso". It's a sad tune but pretty. I don't mind being the daughter of a man who likes a pretty tune. Especially if it's a sad pretty tune. In a way that makes it better. And ...' She raised her voice, edging sharpness. 'Goddammit, I have a right to know!'

'Yes, you do.'

Sarah opened a drawer in her desk, and took out an address book.

'His name's Paul Webster. He was a history student but he dropped out except in those days it was called being sent down. The last I heard of him he was living in the Cotswolds. I'll give you the address. He might still be there but don't bank on it.'

Her voice was cool and controlled. The subversive zest had disappeared. She printed the name and address boldly on a sheet of paper, and handed it to Rachel.

'How come you've got the address? Everybody else tells me either he never existed or he's disappeared off the face of the earth.'

'I'm more efficient than most people. Paul and I traded Christmas cards for quite a few years. Very odd, in the circumstances.' She didn't elaborate. 'Fact of the matter is, I used to send him an annual report. About you. It was a secret arrangement between Paul and me. Not even your mother knew about it. But it all petered out a few years ago. He seemed to lose interest. Sorry. If you manage to find him, don't place your expectations too high.'

'I'll expect nothing. That way I'm bound to be pleasantly surprised.'

There was no response. Sarah sat forward, rested her chin on her hands, and though looking at Rachel, seemed to stare beyond and through her, down the years to that tiny room in the hostel. Her face proclaimed grief of a quality Rachel had not seen in the family.

'Ann was my best friend and she's dead.'

FIVE

Evidence

Will hated the Cotswolds. He found them pretty, and in his architect's vocabulary prettiness was a term of violent abuse. Prettiness put the Cotswolds in the same aesthetic category as Siamese cats, the young Shirley Temple and *The Sound of Music*. He and Rachel had spent their first holiday together camping in the area. He would drink too much cider at lunchtime, then preach at her: 'We should have gone to the Pennines. You look at the hills and the valleys and they're beautiful, but they're also *useful*. You can graze sheep on the hills and there are mills in the valleys that bring forth wool and cotton. Old Lowry, he knew. That's why he painted it. He showed us what the North looked like and why it was important. He wouldn't have wasted his time dragging his easel into the Cotswolds. A sixpenny postcard says it all.'

She heard many outbursts of this kind during their stay, though they eased in their frequency and ferocity when he discovered the length, breadth and texture of a cider hangover.

His passionate concern was fun and it had spiced their holiday; but when Rachel suggested a day trip to the area she discovered the years had not mellowed his attitude.

'The Cotswolds! Who the hell wants to go there?'

'I do.'

'They make me puke.'

'It was the cider that made you puke.'

'The place makes me puke. All those thatched roofs and twee pottery shops. I want to drive a ten-lane motorway through the lot, remind them what real life's all about. Send in a few coach-loads of football supporters. Like a delegation from the twentieth century.'

Rachel tried cool reason and logic. She explained that

her investigations into the identity and whereabouts of her father had ended with the name, Paul Webster, and an address in the Cotswolds. 'If that's where he is, that's where I've got to go.'

'Write a letter. Claim your inheritance. Insist on cash. Used notes.'

'I've already written a letter. I've said I'm coming next Sunday.'

It was Will's turn for reason and logic.

'You can't go on Sunday. We go to your Dad's on Sunday.'

Since her mother's death, the family had developed a new ritual of Sunday lunch at the family home. Rachel and Dawn prepared the meal, the men washed up and they all four meandered the afternoon away, reading the papers, dozing through old movies and football matches on television, talking with forced animation about the government's latest bout of duplicity. It was all designed as healing therapy for John and it showed signs of working. He no longer wandered off to the greenhouse and was able to talk about Ann without breaking off in mid-sentence.

'Dad's getting better. He doesn't need us to go *every* Sunday.'

'But he's bound to ask where you are. And I'll have to tell him.'

Rachel looked at him sharply. It sounded like a coded message.

'That sounds like you're going to send me to the Cotswolds on my own.'

'Only if you absolutely insist on going at all. For God's sake, it's a four-hundred-mile round trip. It's November. You'll get rain and fog. And besides . . .'

She didn't wait for the besides. 'So, on the one hand you don't want me driving all that way on my own. On the other hand you won't come with me. Just because you think the Cotswolds are pretty. You're a good, reasonable man, my love, but sometimes you're a pain in the bottom.'

Their rows were infrequent, and always conducted

63

quietly, as if they felt the need to prove how civilized they were. The murmurs drifted into a silence. Will set up his drawing-board. Rachel read a book. Dawn walked in on them soon after ten o'clock, on her way back from the cinema.

'Hello young lovers, you're under arrest. Any chance of coffee and a lift home?' Then she caught the scent of subdued battle. 'Sorry. Have I interrupted emotional upheavals?'

'You tell her,' said Will, getting up from the drawing-board and going into the kitchen. While he made coffee, Rachel outlined her plans for the following Sunday.

'But you come to us on a Sunday.'

'Just this once you'll have to manage without me.'

'Honestly, you're just like Bugs Bunny.'

Will popped his head around the kitchen door.

'Did you say the woman I love is like Bugs Bunny?'

'Yes.'

'I think I'm entitled to an explanation, since I'm the one you say looks like a rabbit,' said Rachel.

'I didn't say you looked like a rabbit. It's your psychology. I saw this interview with the man who invented Bugs Bunny and he said Bugs is a zealot. Meaning he trebles the effort when he's forgotten the point.'

'But I haven't forgotten the point. The point is to find my real father. I now have his name and address. On Sunday I'm going to see him.'

'In a pretty little thatched cottage in the Cotswolds,' said Will, making his entrance in the manner of a waiter, carrying a tray, with a tea-towel draped over his arm. He put the tray on the coffee-table. He had designed and built it himself. It was sturdy, low-slung, made from pine and not pretty. The waiter act was partly for Dawn's benefit. She enjoyed him showing off, because he wasn't very good at it. It was also an attempt to ease the tension. He hated rows, even if they were quiet. If they were unresolved at bedtime, he would lie awake, trebling the anxiety when he had forgotten the point.

Dawn sipped her coffee and nibbled a fig roll. They

64

carried a permanent stock of fig rolls at the flat, specifically for her late-evening visits.

'Dad's not happy about all this detective work,' she said.

'He hasn't said so to me.'

'He wouldn't, would he? Obviously.'

Rachel held her hands out, palms upstretched, in a gesture of helplessness and frustration.

'What do you want me to do? I haven't made a secret of what I've been doing. I said I wanted to find him and now I'm going to do it. You can't ask me to stop now.'

'Things will change,' said Dawn.

'Of course they will. Things do change. I've heard you complain often enough about everything being in a rut.'

'These last few weeks, I'd have settled for a nice rut.'

They all three recognized the burden of Dawn's complaint. Day by day she shared a house with John, simultaneously sharing his contained grief. Her response was a non-stop chirpiness that passed all understanding, including her own. She kept the shadows at bay most of the time, but when she visited Will and Rachel, she felt secure in allowing the jaunty mask to slip, so that her pain could see the light.

At heart she understood Rachel's need to find her father, but she was an adolescent girl living on a short fuse, and a short time-scale. She had grown to rely on the Sunday visits to spread the load of inverted parental responsibility. It was the one time in the week when it was someone else's turn to keep an eye on John, gently touching the footbrake whenever conversation drifted too close to the precipice of raw memory. Knowing the visits would be resumed a week on Sunday was no sort of consolation. At Dawn's age, ten days could be an eternity.

Rachel got up from her chair and sat down on the floor beside her sister, slipping an arm round her shoulder.

'It's going to sound like patronizing crap, but I do understand.'

'Sure.'

Rachel stretched out her other hand, touching Will on the knee.

'Change the subject, Will. Make us all laugh.'

'I already did my impersonation of a waiter. You ignored that.'

'I've seen you do it better,' said Dawn.

'I'm sorry. I'll try harder next time. I'll wear a pretty frock. I know. You've been to the pictures tonight?'

'Yes.'

'And how did you enjoy the film, Mrs Lincoln?'

'It was great. Clint Eastwood.'

'Killing people?'

'Hundreds. And a car crash every five minutes for comic relief.'

They fell silent again. Car crashes were no longer funny. With a combination of fig rolls, coffee and gentle bodily contact, they tried to make the ghosts behave themselves.

It was still dark when Rachel left the flat for her day trip to the Cotswolds. Will stirred but did not wake. He was a good judge: when the day dawned, south of the Yorkshire border, it dawned murky, and it stayed that way through the Midlands. Her quest seemed sillier with each passing mile. She had set the meter at zero, determined to prove to Will that the round trip was significantly less than the four hundred miles he had estimated. She had it calculated at three hundred and fifty. Even if she were right, it felt like a pathetic attempt to win a trivial victory.

It was over a week since her letter to Paul Webster, at the address given her by Sarah. There had been no reply. As the meter clicked over to show 100 miles, the first rain of the day hazed across the windscreen. Gentle rain from heaven, thought Rachel: I must be getting near Stratford.

She tried to remember the word she had been taught in English lessons – the word describing the trick used by poets when the weather matched the mood of the moment. All she could think of was onomatopoeia but she knew that was wrong. The whole day was wrong, soddit. All the radio programmes were wrong: mile upon mile of

66

unrelenting God-slottery. Though, in theory, a quest for her father was an enterprise with obvious universal overtones, she didn't need spiritual guidance along the way. She needed trivia.

Will, sweetly wise as usual, had anticipated the problem. 'The radio'll be a washout. Nothing but phone-ins to jolly vicars. Take some tapes with you.'

She had brought tapes. Inevitably she had chosen the wrong ones, estimating that on a long journey she would welcome music with substance: Mozart, Brahms, Bruckner, because they were learning about him, and Mahler, because neither of them ever travelled an inch without Mahler. She dipped into the tapes, but was filled with an enormous lust for Ella Fitzgerald, Keith Jarrett, Tom Waits or even Bette Midler. She needed simple, short, upfront life-affirming songs and tunes with an optimum length of three minutes. Music to boil eggs by. Music to shine like a torch beam through the Sunday murk.

The Sunday Murk — a good name for a tabloid, she decided, as the rain fell more heavily, and a phone-in priest moved over, making way for a panel of economists disagreeing with each other about inflation.

Beyond Stratford, Rachel started looking for clues that might lead to her destination. The address was cryptic in the rural manner — Chestnut Cottage, The Lane — a couple of miles from one of the Chippings. It was not the sort of place to find with the aid of map references and road signs. It was the sort of place you found by getting lost, then searching for a human being who might know of a Chestnut Cottage and a Lane in the correct juxtaposition.

Rachel filled up with petrol at a one-pump station with an attendant and no special offers. The man wiped down her windscreen and offered to check her oil. She could tell this was another country. He also knew the way to Chestnut Cottage. All she had to do was remember the correct permutation of left and right turns, and watch out for the war memorial. It was very like life really.

The cottage, when she found it, was neither pretty nor thatched. It was hardly a cottage, but a squat brick-built bungalow with a tiled roof. It was plain ugly. Will would have approved. It was marooned in a small brown field that seemed to be inviting competitive tenders from would-be gardeners. Rachel parked the car in a road that had neither seen nor required white lines, let alone single yellows. She walked up the path. It was inch-deep in mud. She was wearing sensible driving shoes, but obviously this was gumboot territory.

Approaching the door, she reflected this should have been a key moment in her life. It was an occasion for a Wagnerian fanfare, but her main concern was to get out of the rain, together with an earnest hope that pretty Cotswold hospitality would extend to a cup of tea and an invitation to use the lavatory. She wondered whether the cottage had proper drainage or a mains water supply.

There was certainly no doorbell, though she looked very hard at every surface and crevice. She banged on the door with her fist, assuming that was local custom and practice. She half-expected to hear the barking of savage dogs but there was no sound at all. Were they all out milking or shearing or fixing fences? She looked around for signs of animals but all she saw was the murky green foliage of trees and fields and, more cheerfully, a child's swing to one side of the bungalow. She knocked again, jarring her knuckles.

The door opened quietly. There was no noise of bolts being drawn, chains unhooked, or combinations fed into complex locking mechanisms. To be sure, this was another country, where people were not afraid of strangers.

A large man filled the doorway. Rachel's initial reaction was: My God, have I driven a hundred and seventy miles, and a third of a lifetime for this? She was right to have gone easy on the Wagnerian fanfares, though the jeans he was wearing looked of similar vintage to the Ring Cycle. Atop of the jeans an ancient rugby shirt with cherry-and-white hoops fought gallantly to contain a sturdy chest and an overflowing beer belly. He was also, in the memorable words of whichever Oxbridge satirist said it, an hairy man. His face peered through a tangled foliage of hair and beard, like a kid crawling through a hedge in autumn. The hair looked as if it might continue over all his body. Rachel quickly checked his hands and feet in case she'd encountered a werewolf in transit, but they seemed normal though on the large size. If not a werewolf, he must be either a farmer or a folk-singer and possibly both. She could imagine him tramping the hills, a sheep under each arm, then quaffing ale by the quart each evening in between choruses addressed to all ye good shepherds. The visible evidence indicated a man in his late forties. She might have to learn to call him Father.

'Paul Webster?' she said, trying not to sound too wary.

'No. I've drawn a lot of short straws in my time but that isn't one of them.'

It was a warm, educated voice that sounded as if it had started life as untutored Birmingham.

'I was told he lived at this address.'

'I daresay. And Will Shakespeare used to live up the road but he isn't here now. Come on in and tell us about it.'

'Are you sure?'

'It's pissing down and we're both getting cold and wet. Come on in.'

He led her into a large country kitchen, dominated by an Aga stove giving off heat sufficient to warm the entire county and a long wooden-topped table with room to feed a team of haymakers at one end and write a potential Booker prize-winning novel at the other. Both events seemed possible – even imminent.

'I did write a letter,' said Rachel, feeling the need to explain her presence.

'To the aforementioned Paul Webster?'

'Yes.'

'This one?'

He took down a wad of letters, wedged on a shelf between two casseroles, and handed her the one from the top of the pile.

'Yes, that's mine.'

The letter was unopened. Rachel handed it back.

'It's postmarked York,' the man said, as he replaced the letters on the shelf.

'Yes. That's where I live.'

'You've driven all the way from York?'

'Yes.'

'Sit down. I'll make you some coffee. Better still, stay for lunch. Roast beef and Yorkshire. How's that?'

'I can't possibly.'

'Of course you can. I always cook far too much. I also eat far too much. So you'll be doing me two favours.'

'At least let me explain what I'm doing here.'

He filled an old-fashioned whistling kettle and placed it on the hob.

'This explanation you're threatening me with . . . does it relate to the said Paul Webster, late of this parish?'

She nodded.

'Then wait till Gillian's here. It's sure to be a long and complicated story and I don't want to sit through it twice. I try not to scramble my brains on a Sunday, if I can help it. But you'll eat with us?'

'Thank you. You're very kind.'

'I'm famous for it. What's your name? I hate eating with strangers.'

'Rachel. Rachel Harris.'

'I'm Stan. Short for Stanley. After Stanley Matthews. Though I don't suppose that name means much to you. Of course not, you're much too young.'

Rachel warmed to his free-flowing, amiable chat. He seemed a man totally without guile and without venom.

'Who was Stanley Matthews?'

'A legendary footballer. A right-winger. Bear in mind in those days a right-winger was a man who played down the right-hand side of a football pitch. These days it's a man who wants to privatize everything that moves and send the rest of us to prison. Whereas Stanley Matthews was an artist. They called him the Wizard of the Dribble. What a hero. My Dad wanted me to inherit the mantle but I was born fat and got progressively fatter.'

He was a born prattler, who carried his stream of

70

thought close to the surface of his being. As he prattled, he prepared the Yorkshire puddings. He poured hot fat from the meat into baking tins, then added the pudding mixture, before carefully placing the tins in the oven. He moved with precision and the special grace peculiar to certain large people.

'I sometimes wonder whether there's ever been a kid who wasn't a disappointment to his parents. Do you suppose Will Shakespeare's old man really wanted him to have a proper job?' He slid into a yokellish version of the accent Rachel had heard from the man at the filling station. 'Stop thee farting about with they sonnets, young Willum, and get thyself articled to yonder village blacksmith.'

'If you're not the wizard of the dribble, what are you?' said Rachel. She felt safe in asking.

'Guess.'

'When I first saw you, I marked you down as a farmer or a folk singer.'

Stan laughed loudly and thoroughly. The rugby shirt jiggled up and down, revealing a strip of pretty pink flesh.

'That's wonderful. Bloody wonderful.'

'Am I close?'

'I cannot tell a lie. I'm a civil servant. One of the mighty army of faceless bureaucrats.'

'You don't look like a civil servant.'

'Thank you. That's the nicest thing anybody's said to me today. Not that anybody's said very much to me today, this being Sunday. Stop buggering about, Stan, and tell the truth. I work for the county leisure services department. I tramp over the hills and dales, persuading the artisans and peasants they'd like a drop of art after tea. Fellini films in the village hall. Exhibitions of Hockney prints in the scouts' hut. Fringe theatre companies doing one-night stands of two-handed versions of *The Three Sisters*. The usual crap.'

She wasn't fooled by the self-deprecation. The speech had been used before, honed over many a pint, but it was covering for modesty, not cynicism.

'I think you love your work,' said Rachel.

'Ah. You cheated. You were supposed to have your eyes closed while I said all that.'

He was checking his two veg when he turned and crossed to the door, several seconds before it opened.

A woman, not much older than Rachel, came in. She had rust-coloured hair, cropped short, and was dressed similarly to Stan, but her jeans looked marginally post-World-War-Two and the shirt had vertical stripes instead of horizontal hoops. The effect was to make her look about one-third the size of Stan. When he embraced her, she almost disappeared completely, and seemed content to do so.

'Precious jewel of the whole wide world. I missed you.'

'I was only gone half-an-hour.'

'It seemed like a lifetime.'

'Bollocks.'

'Fair comment.'

They unmeshed themselves and Stan made the formal introductions.

'Gillian, this is Rachel. Rachel, this is Gillian.'

Before either of them could say anything, he added his footnotes.

'Gillian is the woman I live with and who lives with me in as much sin as we can manage, bearing in mind we both have demanding jobs with mediocre career prospects. Rachel has travelled the narrow road from the deep North, in search of information about a man called Paul Webster.'

'Leave a space so I can say hello,' said Gillian.

'Sorry. I'll set the table, quietly and without fuss.'

'Hello Rachel.'

'Hello Gillian.'

They hesitated, both looking at Stan.

'I mean it. I'll be totally silent. You get on with your women's talk.'

'I think I should go first,' said Rachel.

'OK. Go ahead.'

'It's tricky, because I assumed somebody would have read my letter.'

'Rachel wrote the letter that arrived last week,' said Stan.

'We still get quite a few letters for Paul. Yours was unusual. Most of them come in envelopes with windows in. Final Demand written in red on the outside . . . that kind of thing.'

'But you don't open them?'

'Of course not. They're for him.'

'Shouldn't you forward them?'

'Difficult to do that without an address.'

Rachel, for her part, suddenly found it difficult to talk openly about her situation. Paul Webster obviously cast a shadow over Gillian's past, but how dark and painful there was no way of telling.

She had walked in on a partnership and shared life-style that even on a few minutes' observation felt very special. Of course, every couple that ever shared a space had its own uniqueness – the boisterous insults that sustained her grandparents, the tranquillity of her own parents and the tenderness she shared with Will. These were all special in their way. But Stan and Gillian appeared to have spanned an age gap of around fifteen years – and, Rachel could not help observing, a weight gap approaching ten stone – with an energy and exuberance she had never seen in any of her family or friends. The bonding was so strong you could almost reach out and touch it. Each anticipated the other's movements and needs with uncanny accuracy and perception. It was a rare and beautiful boat and she did not want to rock it.

Gillian near enough read her thoughts. 'Can I make it easier for you?' she said.

'Maybe you could. You're giving me roast beef and Yorkshire. I don't want to say anything that might upset either of you. It's a lousy way to repay hospitality.'

'She was a stranger and we took her in,' said Stan, opening the oven door and beaming on his triumphant puddings therein.

'Look at that! Come and have a look, both of you. Did you ever see such a sight? Oh, what a piece of work is

73

Stan!' He closed the oven door. 'Another five minutes, then we'll eat, and you can tell Rachel the story of your life with the Apostle Paul.'

'He's part of my past,' said Gillian. 'Is he part of yours?'

'Yes. But not in the same way.'

Over lunch, which had all the splendour promised by its cook, Gillian spoke about Paul.

'I met him six years ago. We came here to live five years ago. He left me four years ago. All to the nearest month.'

'And I moved in two years ago, if you're interested,' added Stan.

'I'm really interested in Paul,' said Rachel.

'In that case, pass me the rest of the potatoes and I'll shut up.'

'He must be quite a bit older than you,' Rachel said.

'She likes the maturity and stability of older men. Sorry. I promised to shut up.'

Gillian laughed. 'Paul! Mature and stable!'

'Immature and unstable?' asked Rachel.

'You bet. He left me just after his forty-second birthday and he was still behaving like a teenager. That's to say, trying to behave like a teenager. It doesn't really work.'

'I behave like a six-year-old. That works.'

This time both the women ignored Stan. He seemed happy enough with the arrangement, as with their tacit approval he cut himself another slice of beef and neatly shovelled the remaining roast potatoes on to his plate.

'Paul was always full of surprises. That's what I liked about him.' Gillian amended the statement. 'It's what I *loved* about him. He'd go out and I'd ask him where he was going. He'd put his fingers to his lips and say "Misterioso".'

' "Misterioso"? It's a tune.'

'Oh yes, I know that. A blues, constructed out of walking sixths. He used to play it for me.'

'The record?'

'No. On the saxophone. He played alto. He didn't really want to be Paul Webster. He wanted to be Charlie Parker, or Johnny Hodges, or Dexter Gordon, or John Coltrane.

He wanted to be anybody except Paul Webster.'

'You should tell Rachel, he isn't really Paul Webster anyway,' said Stan.

'You'll have to explain that.'

'When we lived together, occasionally he'd get letters addressed to him under other names. Paul Webster, Paul Carney, Paul Hodges. When I asked him about it, he said he always carried a few spare names for reasons of personal convenience. And he only used the names of great jazz saxophone players.'

'Why should he have more than one name?'

'When I asked him he put his fingers to his lips and said . . .'

Rachel finished the sentence for her. ' "Misterioso"?'

'Right.'

'It's a nice tune. Sad but pretty.'

Rachel could hear it in her mind and, looking at Gillian, she guessed she could hear it too. She was digging in memory now and, as if in deference, Stan left the table and started to make coffee.

'Every time he went out I'd ask him where he was going. He'd say "Misterioso" and he'd come back later with flowers or a bottle of champagne or a dog.'

'A dog?'

'The sweetest little puppy you ever saw. I still don't know where he got it. The little ball of fluff grew up into an Irish wolfhound. The size of an elk.'

Rachel looked around the room. 'I see no elk.'

'He's in the back yard wallowing in the slime,' said Stan. 'As soon as he hears me clearing the table, he'll crash his way through the door, demanding food.'

'You're all right with dogs?' asked Gillian.

'The bigger the better.'

'Good.'

Gillian smiled at secret thoughts of puppy-dog tales. Then the smile faded. Stan moved around the room, and stood behind her, a hand resting on her shoulder. Again he knew what she was going to say before she said it, as if the echo came first.

'One day he was going out. I asked him where he was going. He said . . . "Misterioso". I haven't seen him since.'

Stan put both arms around her and gave her a big hug.

She reassured Rachel. 'It's all right. It doesn't hurt. Not now.'

'Do you have any idea where he went?'

'He wrote to me with a forwarding address in London. About eighteen months ago, the letters started coming back. Not known at this address. And since he's no longer known at this address, we have a small stack of letters with his name on. Various of his names.'

Over coffee, Gillian said: 'May I have a turn now?'

'Sure.'

'Why do you want to know about Paul?'

'Because he was at university with my mother and I'm pretty sure he's my father.'

They were both stunned by Rachel's words. They listened intently as she told them of her mother's death and the investigation that had brought her to the Cotswolds on a wet Sunday lunchtime. When she finished, Gillian said: 'Jesus Christ.'

'I'll tell you the really awful part,' said Stan. 'When Rachel knocked at the door, and I opened it, she must have thought for one terrible moment that I was Daddy.'

It broke the tension and they all three laughed at the thought.

Rachel owned up. 'I did. It was a nasty moment. I'm not so sure now. I think you'd make a very good Daddy.'

'Alas and alack, not true. I tried it. I screwed it up. That's another story. Gillian's scar tissue's in better shape than mine.' He shrugged an apology for the sudden show of vulnerability. 'Scratch any Falstaff and you'll find a whining little Hamlet with a lorry-load of hangups.'

Now Gillian became the bringer of strength, reaching across the table, grasping his hands and kissing both of them. A television soap opera would have added synthesized violins and an angel choir. Done silently and with a relative stranger as the sole witness, it was simple and touching. Love of this kind was a sign of strength, and a

76

price had been paid by both partners. In a dentist's waiting-room Rachel had once read that if you broke an arm or a leg, properly treated the limb would become stronger around the area of the fracture. She had reported this to Will, in the cosy euphoria of two complicated fillings survived with dignity. He had said: 'So what? You can't build your life on what you pick up from *Reader's Digest*.'

The incident lingered, an irritant in her mind. It was stupid to moan about contentment and the peaceful passing of the days; but real passion with the depth and strength and urgency demonstrated by Gillian and Stan seemed to be tied inevitably to pain and the shedding of blood. Could you have a Dunkirk spirit without a Dunkirk? Maybe she should write to *Reader's Digest* and ask them.

It was after five in the afternoon when Rachel set off on the journey north. They had spent the afternoon drinking tea at hourly intervals, while Gillian talked about Paul. As predicted, the wolfhound made an exuberant entrance at the sound of plates being stacked on the draining board. He was a cheerful beast, big enough to saddle up and ride from Ghent to Aix, with or without good news. He would have made the trip for the sheer joy of using up surplus energy. Around four o'clock, Rachel's hosts had insisted she should have a nap before the return journey. They had made her comfortable on a settee in the living room, and covered her with a rug.

She asked: 'Where's my Teddy Bear?' Stan had smiled: 'I'm the resident Teddy Bear and I'm spoken for.'

But he had tucked her in and woken her an hour later with a cup of tea.

Driving into the darkness, she still felt enveloped by the warmth of their welcome, and the hugs and kisses on departure. At times she had almost forgotten the real reason for her visit but now she recalled fragments of Gillian's conversation, trying to fit them into a pattern.

'Paul — he was a dreamer. When we came here, we were

77

going to be a self-sufficient community. We'd grow food in the garden and open a shop in the village selling pots to the tourists. He knew lots of people who made pots. The important thing was time. You must always be in control of time. Otherwise time gets in control of you . . .

'He needed time for his music. He used to practise a lot, I'll give him credit for that. Hour after hour. If we'd had neighbours they'd have complained. Not everybody wants to hear "Lester Leaps In" twenty-seven times on the trot, even if it's jazz and every time different . . .

'The year we were together, he never earned a penny. Eventually I took a job in Stratford. Souvenir shop, selling junk to the Americans. Ophelia ball-point pens and Dunsinane ashtrays. But I didn't mind. He had his dreams and he believed them and he made me believe them too. Trouble was, they changed every Thursday . . .

'What did he look like? Dark hair, slightly built, angular, a lot of energy, nervous energy, always in a hurry to get on with the next thing, even if he didn't know what it was. Travelling desperately, he once said. It's better to travel desperately than to arrive . . .

'I don't know why he used different names. Well, I guessed it was partly because people were chasing him for money. Most of the letters came from banks and credit-card companies and such like. The envelopes with the windows in. But he always said he never borrowed money from people, only from institutions. He wasn't crazy about institutions. He thought people were wonderful. He thought institutions were lousy . . .

'The dreams? What were they? Oh, all kinds of crazy ideas. For a start, he wanted to be the greatest alto sax player since Charlie Parker, but he knew he couldn't do that. So it was I think I'll write a novel . . . open an art gallery . . . have a jazz club . . . the hell with it, I'll do all three . . . And like I say, he meant it, until the following Thursday came around . . .

'Where is he? Probably London but I can't give you any evidence . . .

'What is he about? Trying to make the world match his

dreams, I suppose, in the sure and certain knowledge that it can't be done. Travelling desperately . . .

'And Rachel, love, I don't know if this is what you want to hear, but in his quiet moments he was very like you, and you are very like him . . . '

Will was waiting up for her.

'Any joy?' he asked.

'Yes, lots of joy.'

'You found him?'

'No. I didn't find him. That looks like a dead end. Lost without trace. No forwarding address. But I found lots of joy.'

SIX

Air-Conditioned Jungle

Christmas was the cruellest day.

According to long tradition, John and Ann had always played host and hostess, providing food, drink and shelter. Rachel and Dawn organized silly games. Grandma Jackson was resident critic and Grandpa Jackson smoked his pipe, gritting his teeth against the taste of whatever tobacco Dawn had given him as a present. She thought he was too conservative in his tastes and tried, every year and totally without success, to expand his perception.

Without Ann, there was a subtle re-allocation of roles and responsibilities. Rachel prepared the meal, with noisy assistance from her grandmother, Dawn was in charge of the silly games and, while John remained chief wine waiter, Will took everyone by surprise, Rachel included, by producing three bottles of champagne as a supplement to the house white.

'Don't reckon much to it. Too gassy. Like bottled beer. Bloody bubbles get right up your nose,' said Grandpa Jackson, holding out his glass for a refill.

By early evening, everyone had passed through the healing stupor following the over-eating, and Dawn announced this year's silly game. She had really wanted to play Trivial Pursuit, but all her friends at school were into Trivial Pursuit and she was a dedicated student of fashion: she studied which way it was going and headed quickly in a different direction. She had found a game that combined the elements she wanted – pushing plastic counters around a board and asking pointless questions – but in a different wrapper. For all practical purposes it remained the most trivial of pursuits, but her integrity remained untarnished.

The men played the women. Rachel, flanked by Dawn

and Grandma Jackson, faced John across the blue-checked board with its plastic counters to indicate the ebb and flow of battle. There were dice as well. As happened annually, Dawn tried to explain the rules to the grandparents, ending on a note of hopeful despair saying: 'You'll soon pick it up when we get started.'

Rachel remembered a discussion with Will, some months earlier, when they had stayed up until two o'clock in the morning of a working day watching an epic snooker match, even though neither of them was very interested in snooker. They had agreed that the way people played games was a mercilessly accurate definition of character. The names of Davis and Higgins, Thorburn and White, had been quoted in evidence. It seemed very profound stuff at two o'clock in the morning but wisely they had gone to bed and forgotten all about it. It was odd that she should remember the conversation now, as she put a trivial question to the man opposite.

'Up to what proportion of their own weight can camels drink water?'

'We don't have camels where we live. Ask me a question about football,' said Grandpa Jackson.

'You have to answer this question,' said Rachel.

'Try to visualize a camel,' said Will. 'A camel's the one with two humps, therefore its water capacity is probably greater than a dromedary's which, as we know, only has one hump. Unless the converse is true.'

Grandpa Jackson's pipe had gone out. He drew on it, making juicy gurgling noises, and grumbled: 'It's a daft bloody game this one, our Dawn. Why can't we have carpet bowls like we did last year?'

Dawn grumbled back at him: 'You only liked carpet bowls because you were good at it. And so you should be, you play all summer. It's our turn this year.'

John, who had been silent, suddenly asked: 'Could you repeat the question please, Rachel?'

'Up to what proportion of their own weight can camels drink water?'

'Either twice their own weight or a gallon, whichever is the greater,' said Will.

'That's a load of cobblers and I agree,' said Grandpa Jackson, wandering over to the fireplace to clean out his pipe in the grate.

'Is that your answer?' said Rachel.

'No,' said John firmly.

He was determined to give it greater thought, delving in the recesses of his subconscious for any stray information about the drinking habits of camels.

It was a repeating pattern throughout the game. Rachel would ask a question: 'Which European country's parliament dates from 930 A.D. and is claimed to be the oldest in the world?'; Grandpa Jackson would make rude noises with his pipe and complain about the daftness of the game; Will would offer some ludicrous hypothesis like 'Oldham'; and John would ponder endlessly and earnestly before offering any kind of response. Some of his answers were right, though Will's scattershot approach was the more effective.

For the first time since her mother's death, Rachel found John irritating. They had given him affection and support during the difficult autumn weeks and she felt they deserved something better than boredom in return. That, without question, was the nature of his behaviour. He was boring. She knew these thoughts were unworthy and unfair, but it was a fact of Christmas Day – the one day in the year when families were locked together, nose-to-nose – that tensions floated to the surface.

They were all too polite to say anything and that made the atmosphere worse, though Rachel was more sensitive to it than the others. Dawn allowed herself an occasional 'Hurry up, Dad, it'll soon be Christmas.' But even she soon tired of her own joke, such as it was.

It was while John was pondering yet again, this time over the question: 'How many miles of blood vessels are there in the average man?', that another memory drifted into Rachel's mind. She suddenly heard Gillian's voice, echoing from her Cotswold kitchen a couple of months earlier, saying: 'And Rachel, love, I don't know if this is what you want to hear, but in his quiet moments he was very like you, and you are very like him . . .'

She would always have love and affection for this man called John, who was sitting opposite her, playing a trivial game in a boring way, but she realized more clearly than ever before that she was not *like* him. She was like a man called Paul who dreamed dreams and played a saxophone and travelled desperately under a variety of names; a man who would pursue trivialities to the end of the earth and beyond. The thousands of miles of his blood vessels had fed and nourished hers and the blood line was a mercilessly accurate definition of character.

Early in the New Year, Rachel raised the question of a winter holiday with Joan. Joan, as usual, responded in a brisk and practical manner.

'You'd like the money now? Cash down?'

It was understood that, although the terms of Rachel's unwritten contract with Glenn Travel included one week's winter holiday, she never took the time off, and received an extra week's pay in lieu.

'I thought I might take the holiday this year,' said Rachel.

'You don't *take* your winter holiday. You take the money. That's how the system operates.'

'I'm sorry, Joan. This year, I'd like to take a week off.'

'But it's our busy time.'

It was true. As soon as the Christmas rush was over, the colour supplements and television commercials focussed people's minds unrelentingly on sun-drenched summer beaches with subliminal promises of exotic sex, guarantees of time to pay and postively no extras, providing the pound sterling stayed free of wobbles between January and July.

'I know it's the busy time but . . .'

Rachel hesitated. Joan filled in the blank spaces.

'You want to go looking for your father again. Is that it?'

83

Rachel had provided Joan with edited highlights of her trip to the Cotswolds, on the simple premise that it was impossible to work side by side with a woman such as this and retain any secrets that mattered a damn. Joan never snooped. She just asked, straight out, no messing.

'Yes,' said Rachel, 'I want to go looking for my father.'

'In London?'

'That's where he was going when he left Gillian. It's the obvious place to go.'

'From everything you've told me, the guy's a shit. There are ten million shits in the naked city and he is one of them. Is it worth a week's wages, I ask myself.'

'But you think all men are shits.'

'No I don't. There are exceptions.'

Joan started counting, silently, on her fingers.

'It's always the same. I get stuck at three which, I'm told, is not statistically significant. So yes, all men are shits and a thousand pounds to a used Kleenex says your old man is another.'

'May I have a week's holiday so I can try to prove it? Or disprove it? Whichever?'

'On one condition.'

'What's the condition?'

Joan's telephone rang. She picked up the receiver.

'Glenn Travel. Mr Bannister, my word, this is a nice surprise!'

She made a face at Rachel. Though a dedicated client and traveller, Mr Bannister was also a member of a fringe religious sect and prefaced most conversations with extensive quotes, generally from the Book of Revelations. Leaflets followed by first-class post. Joan covered the mouthpiece knowing time was on her side.

'The condition of you taking a week's holiday is you book your travel and accommodation through Glenn Travel.'

Rachel's telephone rang.

'And you'd better do it quickly. It's our busy time.'

* * *

84

Will was understanding, in his specially quiet and solicit-
ous manner, indicating that though he understood, he
thought the idea barmy.

'Would you like me to come with you?' he said.

'Why?'

He sat at his drawing-board, doing overtime on a water-
colour perspective of the Old People's Home. The
management committee had asked for a proper drawing
because its members couldn't understand plans and eleva-
tions. Will resented doing unnecessary work for visual
illiterates. He picked up a pencil and doodled a dog having
a pee on the corner of the building. Then he answered
Rachel's question.

'If I came with you, I could help. Do your secretarial
work. Act as a minder if you have to go down any mean
streets. Keep watch on suspects until the police arrive. All
the things Watson did for Holmes.'

'You're talking rubbish, dear.'

'I know.'

He rubbed out the dog doodle. The committee would
probably prefer an elegant and caring couple looking like
two of their members on a tour of inspection. It was a
shame. He wondered about drawing some old people
playing five-a-side soccer. Like most architects, he could
only think with a pencil in his hand, even if the subject
was rationalizing about an apparently pointless trip to
London.

'I'll offer you another deal,' he said. 'No rubbish this
time. We both go to London. You do your detective work.
I go to art galleries. Zap up the visual perception. Fill my
head with art. We're supposed to be interested in art in
my trade. As far as that goes, I *am* interested in art. How's
that for a proposition? Then in the evenings we can go to
theatres and concerts. Grab a few slices of Mahler.'

'No.'

'No?'

'No,' she said, more firmly this time.

'Isn't that rather negative?'

'Of course it's negative. It's supposed to be negative. It

isn't that I don't want you to come with me. It's just that I have to go on my own.'

Will sketched in the outlines of a caring, but not overly elegant couple. He needed a pause to pick his way through Rachel's logic. She would like him with her, but also wanted to go on her own. There was a contradiction lurking there somewhere, but she always coped more easily with contradictions than he did. Maybe the missing father was to blame.

'Do I take it,' he said slowly, 'that what you need is an area of personal time, space and privacy, so you can redefine your essential being?'

She picked up a cushion and threatened to throw it at him.

'Throw it at me, not at the drawing!' he said, with a trace of professional panic.

'Get up and move away from the drawing-board.'

He did as he was told, and also moved nearer to her, offering an easy target. She threw the cushion. He allowed it to hit him at waist level, then dropped melodramatically in a heap.

'It won't work,' she said.

Will groaned.

'I've lived through it too many times.'

'What have you lived through too many times?'

'You pretend to be hurt. I come and make you better. You make a miraculous recovery and it all turns into sex.'

'It sounds to me like a very acceptable arrangement,' said Will, who groaned again, clasped his belly in pain and rolled over on his side. 'I really need to be made better.'

Rachel got up from her armchair, walked across to him then knelt down, cradling his head in her arms.

'Better?'

'I'm starting to get a little bit better but it still hurts when I laugh.'

She kissed him softly and at length, then said: 'You will soon feel very much better. But I am still going to London. And I am going on my own. And if you say one more word about personal space I shall draw bottoms and willies all over your Old People's Home.'

According to Joan Glenn's highly personal scale, Rachel's hotel was worth 3¾ stars, and she was paying 2¼-star rates, a profit margin to the consumer of 1½ stars. It was a modern building on the western edge of Bloomsbury, dating from the 1960s. The brochure, inevitably, sang the praises of its clean lines, meaning it was an ugly concrete box with faded pink panels making a feeble gesture towards the spectrum. It would never look properly old, in the manner of the great old railway hotels, but was destined to look shop-soiled and slightly used until such time as the real-estate men demolished it in favour of some hi-tech alternative.

Rachel's room was large and light, again with clean modern lines, meaning the ceiling, walls and floors were all flat and met at right angles to each other. She had as many mod cons as she could learn to use in a week: kettle, remote-control television, tea and coffee bags, refrigerated drinks cabinet and an in-house video facility that she guessed was a euphemism for dirty movies. She might try one later in the week though she was lukewarm about Swedes and gymslips.

It was the first time she had stayed in an hotel on her own and the first time she had been to London on her own. It was bliss to waste time over trivialities. She spent an hour having a bath and washing her hair and another hour hanging up her clothes. She plucked up enough courage to ring room service and order tea and biscuits. When they arrived, she lay on the bed, half-dressed, drinking tea and watching afternoon television, switching between an Australian soap opera and a home-made game show with a combined mental age of around seven.

York seemed like another planet. She had boarded the train at ten o'clock that morning, with a head full of plans for the metropolitan quest. Now she could hardly remember what any of the plans were, apart from the central principle of finding her father, and even that was beginning to feel like a task for tomorrow. She found herself reciting the lines she had learned for O Level Eng. Lit.:

Surely, surely, slumber is more sweet than toil, the shore
Than labour in the deep mid-ocean, wind and wave and
    oar;
Oh rest ye, brother mariners, we will not wander more.

Good old Alfred Lord, he knew what he was talking about. There was no doubt about it. Slumber beat the hell out of toil. Ring room service: send me a treble lotos on the rocks and I'll have an early morning call a week tomorrow.

When she woke, it was dark outside. She looked at her watch. It was seven o'clock. Seven o'clock of a dark January evening and all's torpid. She felt a brief pang of tourist guilt. The night-life and glamour of London's West End were girding their loins out there. In a hundred dressing-rooms great actors and actresses were preparing to give memorable performances in award-winning plays of great significance. Symphony orchestras were checking their reeds and fine-tuning their bow-ties. Alternative comedians were brushing up on their ad libs and waiters were preparing tables in a thousand grill rooms, bistros and pizza joints. And I want no part of it, thought Rachel.

I am not a tourist. I am not on a cheap package tour from Macclesfield or Milwaukee. I am a free woman, pursuing my own destiny, and I need no artificial aids.

She decided to telephone Will, so she could tell him how much she was enjoying her independence. There was no reply and she remembered he was out at a conservation meeting. A developer wanted to chop down some trees and Will wanted to stop him. She hung up. A pile of fat telephone directories lay on a bedside shelf. She thought: Webster. I am here to find a man believed to be called Paul Webster.

She picked up the volume marked S–Z and opened it to the letter W. This was the way to be a private detective; lounging on a bed in an air-conditioned room, with a telephone and room service when required. Tennyson's mariners would have approved though the poet himself, who always struck Rachel as an austere sort of chap, would probably have curled an admonishing lip.

There were four columns of Websters. She decided to count them. There were approximately one hundred and thirty-seven to each column. She reached into her handbag for the pocket calculator Will had put in her Christmas stocking. She had been longing to use it, preferably on something pointless, and this felt right. Four columns of Websters at one hundred and thirty-seven per column came to five hundred and forty-eight. It was well worth writing down in her book, even though it was irrelevant to her task. It came under the general heading of what Grandpa Jackson always called: sizing up the job. In his world-view, no job should be undertaken unless it had been properly sized up.

Theoretically, she could simplify the task by concentrating on the name Paul. About thirty of the Websters had the initial P, but so what? His real name might be J Paul Webster, like the Getty of not quite the same name. In her hermetically-sealed cell, she was content to meander, dream-like, filling her mind and notebook with trivia, and rehearsing the odd speech.

'Hello, you don't know me, and this is going to sound totally ludicrous but are you by any chance the Paul Webster who was at Leeds University in 1959? If so, I am your long-lost daughter. And if not, please accept my most sincere apologies if this has caused you any embarrassment.'

Even if by some mathematical fluke she rang the right number, she might find herself talking to Paul Webster's wife, lover, son or daughter. She could end up saying: 'I am your long-lost half-sister.'

It was not necessarily the kind of message impressionable young people wanted to receive on a Monday evening between 'Coronation Street' and 'Brookside'.

She thought: Hodges and Carney. These were two of the other pseudonyms Gillian had mentioned. All the same practical objections applied but Rachel was, by now, totally absorbed in a trance of meaningless activity. Time was, for once, *not* of the essence, and she was determined to waste every last second.

She delved into the A-D and E-K volumes, in pursuit of Carney and Hodges. The excitement was starting to pall and she no longer counted the names with her first fine careless zeal. Precision gave way to approximation. At the end of the exercise, she summarized the investigation in her Philip Marple notebook.

> *London Telephone Directory Name Check*
> Websters – 548
> Carneys – 100 approx.
> Hodges – 340 approx.
> Hodge – 200 approx.
> Total: 1148

The confusion over Hodge and Hodges was caused by an inability to read her own handwritten report of the conversation with Gillian. Had she been a jazz buff, she would have known which of the two was the name of the famous saxophone player but she was not and she did not.

She looked at what she had done and thought: this is bloody silly. You are not going to make 1148 telephone calls to total strangers. You are not going to make any phone calls at all. You are going to close this section of the investigation, classify it as sizing up the job, draw a line across the page and clear the bed of all these telephone directories.

Stacking the directories in their architect-designed, clean-lined cubby-hole, she discovered the Yellow Pages. A 'Thinks' bubble popped about six inches above her head. If Paul were still a dedicated musician he would obviously want people to know about it. He would advertise his wares in the market place.

She opened the Yellow Pages to the letter M and found the category headed 'Musicians (SEE ALSO ENTERTAINERS)' She was surprised to find only about thirty names listed, including one man with his name in twice, a pair of chamber orchestras and a bagpipe agency. None of the names bore any resemblance to Webster, Carney, Hodges or Hodge. She checked the Entertainers but they were mostly conjurers and clowns with twee names, hustling on the kids' birthday-party circuit.

None of that was worth writing in her notebook. She put it back in her handbag, along with the pocket calculator. It was now eight-thirty, too late to catch any significant culture in theatre and concert-hall. That was a relief. Deciding what to see would have taken just as long as analysing the telephone directories.

She got up from the bed, her first venture into the vertical plane since the middle of the afternoon. There was a large, double-glazed picture window. It had no obvious handles or hinges. She guessed it was like the windows on the train. Nobody was allowed to open them, because the air-conditioned air provided scientifically within was better for you than the old-fashioned stuff hanging around outside. Windows, seemingly, were strictly for looking through, so she looked through it.

The lights of the city sparkled. She cast around for a Chandleresque image. Like a cheap necklace on an ageing streetwalker? Too sexist. Like fireflies on a tropical beach? Too cute – and fireflies probably lived inland anyway. Like a myriad tiny beacons tempting sailors to a rocky shore? Back to the mariners again.

Still, and all, the lights were sparkling, and there was a whisper of temptation out there, and a bigger range of possibilities than she was used to: fifty-seven varieties of deadly sin though she would probably end up settling for a pizza. She had not eaten since her afternoon tea and biscuits and her constitution was demanding junk food and quickly.

Riding down in the lift it crossed her mind that she could combine gluttony with business. According to her received mythology, London was chock-a-block with shady dives where food of a sort was served, and musicians wearing dark glasses played shady, low-down music. It could be the whole jumbled imagery was a careless mix of scenes from late-night B movies but, true to the style of the thought, it was worth checking out.

She consulted the porter behind the desk in the hotel lobby, wondering idly whether he would have been called a bellhop had the setting been Los Angeles.

'Excuse me,' she said, suddenly hearing her own voice as terribly, terribly English, 'I wonder if you could suggest any places nearby where I might hear some jazz. And find something to eat.'

'Jazz?'

He seemed unfamiliar with the word. He was a bright-eyed young man, smartly dressed in a dark green uniform designed to match the hotel's colour scheme and corporate image. English was not his first language. Rachel had a feeling it wasn't even in the first three.

'I would like to eat somewhere pleasant and listen to some music at the same time,' she said slowly, enunciating clearly. She hoped by broadening the specification from jazz in particular to music in general, she might ease his burden of responsibility in a strange land.

'You want jazz,' he said, frowning a little, with no sign of having heard her explanatory paragraph. He fingered his way through a pile of railway and airline timetables on his desk. Had he misunderstood? Did he think jazz was on the way to Scotland or Singapore? She began to regret the whole thing. She wanted to go out and come in again, with a different script.

'Jazz,' he said, with a smile of modest triumph, handing her a copy of *City Limits*.

'Thank you.'

'You find the jazz on page forty-nine, I think.'

'That's wonderful.'

Rachel took the magazine and sat down in the lobby, a safe distance from the porter's desk. Though he apparently knew ten times better than she what was going on behind the sparkling lights of the big city, she was keen to retain her independence of thought and freedom of choice.

The magazine listed in comprehensive detail every permutation of deadly sin available to metropolitan

92

sophisticates, with a keen emphasis on radical politics and health food. Rachel was so intrigued by some of the marginal eccentricities that it was only when the porter called out to her, 'You find some jazz, yes?' that she remembered what she was supposed to be looking for.

'Yes,' she replied, swiftly improvising, 'it's just a question of where to go and what sort.'

She turned to page forty-nine, which was headed: 'MUSIC — JAZZ AND IMPROVISED'. That seemed like a contradiction. From what she remembered of Will's brief lectures on the subject, the whole point of jazz *was* improvisation. If it wasn't improvised it wasn't jazz. She would ask him about it when she returned home.

Under the sub-heading 'MONDAY, she scanned the evening's attractions. Various bands and musicians she had never heard of were playing at Ronnie Scott's, the Pizza Express, the 100 Club, the Bull's Head, the Club Misterioso . . .'

It was like those moments in Tom and Jerry cartoons when the cat suddenly realizes it has galloped off the edge of a precipice ten thousand feet up — the moment of frozen mid-air disbelief prior to the fall, with the velocity and sound-effects of a dive-bomber, followed in its turn by total and instant recovery.

Rachel read the listing in detail.

'Mike Daley, Club Misterioso, ring for details. Piano player and lowdown dirty bopper illuminates brave new underworld jazz spot in darkest Paddington.'

She tried not to be too excited. Simply because her itinerant father had spent his life murmuring 'Misterioso' before disappearing on cryptic errands, sometimes never to return, it did not automatically follow that he would open a jazz club of that name in darkest Paddington. Even so, it had his style, as described by Gillian in the darkest Cotswolds. She decided to act like a mature, grown-up woman. She rang for details, from a pay-phone at the side of the lobby. As she heard the ringing tone she wondered about asking for a precise definition of a lowdown dirty bopper.

'Club Misterioso, can I help you?'

It was a young woman's voice, classless with a hint of Cockney lightly brushed on, as recommended for continuity announcers on Channel 4.

'I was wondering what time things start happening tonight.'

'What time can you get here?'

There was laughter at the other end of the line, suggesting the young woman was playing to a gallery, and beyond that the sound of piano music. It sounded fairly clean.

'Sorry,' said the voice, 'we've got some merchant bankers in tonight. I really am here to give accurate and helpful information.'

Rachel was puzzled by the presence of merchant bankers in lowdown darkest Paddington but filed the question for future reference.

'If I come down to the club, will I be able to get something to eat?'

'It's an open question, to be honest. Yes, we serve food. Our slogan is, ten thousand flies can't be wrong. It isn't original, we stole it from Ronnie. But it captures the spirit, if you see what I mean.'

Rachel did not see what she meant. She had only understood about fifty per cent of the conversation so far.

'Thanks. I may drop in later.'

She tried to sound cool and casual, though she felt alien and provincial, adrift in an exclusive club with her vowel sounds showing, intimidated by the references to flies and Ronnie. The laughing people at the other end of the line were the keepers of a faith forbidden to passing citizens from the land north of the Humber.

'We look forward to seeing you. Do you know how to find us?'

The tone of voice, as throughout, was warm and friendly. It was only her words that occasionally made no sense.

'I'm sure I'll be able to find you. I work for a travel agent.'

This provoked laughter at the other end. Perhaps cute

one-liners were legal tender in Paddington. Gaining confidence, Rachel decided to throw in a curve ball. She was sure that was the phrase she had read in Robert B. Parker.

'Will Paul be around?'

'Paul?'

Rachel had her escape route planned. If the young woman denied the presence of anyone called Paul, she would mumble an apology along the lines of: 'Sorry, I must be confusing us with two other people.'

For the moment she persisted: 'Yes, Paul. Dark-haired guy. Some kind of saxophone player.'

'My orders are to say it depends whether he owes you any money.'

'No. He doesn't owe me any money. He's a sort of a friend from way back.'

'He certainly goes a long way back. Yes, he'll be around. Just lift up his stone and he'll be there.'

'Good. Thanks a lot.'

'You're welcome. We'll see you later?'

She left a query hanging on the end of the sentence, as if expecting that the accurate and helpful information, so freely given, was more likely to deter customers than attract them.

'I'll be along. Put some gin on a low light.'

She smiled to herself as she heard the girl's laughter and sent silent thanks to poor, lonely, drunken Helen for the use of the line. It perpetuated something though God knew what. She hung up the receiver. Though she worked in a travel agency, sending people around the world every day of the week, she had no idea how to get to downtown Paddington. It was another job for the bellhop.

She took the Underground to Paddington and a taxi from there to the Club Misterioso. The hotel porter had recommended it, as the ideal combination of speed, economy and personal security. He seemed to think Rachel needed protection from the city. He had spotted her vulnerability across the lobby from the first minute.

The taxi driver had never heard of the club and took a

little persuading that it existed. Once they found the street, he viewed it warily: 'Are you sure you wouldn't rather go to the pictures, love?'

'No thank you. This is the place.'

'It's your life to live, sweetheart. That'll be two pounds.'

She suspected he had decided it was a lesbian club, and was keen to be away before it could corrode his East End machismo. The taxi drove away leaving the street in almost total darkness. The only light source was the small illuminated plastic sign above the entrance to the club. The door was solid and close-boarded, almost an exact replica of the door to Chestnut Cottage. She pushed it. Nothing happened. There was a brief moment of panic before she read the 'PULL' painted alongside the handle. She pulled on the handle and the door opened.

A short flight of uncarpeted concrete stairs led down to an entrance lobby. A table and chair stood beside an archway leading into the main area of the club. As if sensing her arrival, a young woman walked through from the club and sat down at the table, waiting for her. She wore designer jeans, a sweatshirt bearing the words CLUB MISTERIOSO and a badge with her name on. According to this her name was Pat. She was of an age with Rachel, a chunky and cheerful girl.

As Rachel approached the table, Pat smiled at her.

'A table for one or is *he* outside parking the car?'

'I'm on my own. And there's plenty of parking space.'

Pat tore off a ticket from a roll.

'That'll be three pounds. It's only a small rip-off and I'll hang your coat up for no extra charge.'

She helped Rachel off with her coat, and hung it in a lobby off the entrance. Rachel picked up the ticket from the table.

'Do I need to keep the ticket?'

'Some people save them. When they've got ten, it proves they've been to the club ten times.'

'I'll keep it. If I enjoy myself, I'll start saving them.'

'It's the lady from the travel agency, isn't it?' said Pat. Rachel nodded. Confronted with an open and candid face instead of a distant voice, Rachel felt safe in saying: 'I didn't understand some of the things you said.'

Pat seemed puzzled. 'What didn't you understand?'

'Merchant bankers. You said you had some merchant bankers in tonight. I didn't understand that.'

'It's rhyming slang. People who make a noise instead of listening to the music.'

'Oh, you mean wankers?'

'But ladies don't use language like that.'

'They do where I live.'

'They do where I live too, but we sometimes have to pretend.'

Pat realized that Rachel, having paid her money, abandoned her coat to the care of the management and taken her ticket, had no idea where to go or what to do. She was immediately alert with accurate and helpful information.

'Now, are you going to drink in the bar, have something to eat or listen to the music?'

'I'd like something to eat. I'd also like to listen to the music.'

'Easy. Walk this way, madam.'

'I know, and we're both supposed to limp.'

'Let's not bother.'

Rachel followed her through a crowded bar into a small room set with circular tables and bentwood chairs. There was space for about sixty people, sitting comfortably. There were nine people present. The stage was at the same level as the audience. a quartet was playing, made up of saxophone, piano, bass and drums. The music was throbbing, plangent and, to Rachel's ears, selectively discordant. Every fifth note seemed to be wrong, but wrong to a deliberate pattern and purpose. She sat alone at a table near the band, though, by definition, every table was near the band. After a while, the wrong notes began to seem right. They were an integral part of the atmosphere.

Each table had a candle in a wine bottle encrusted with wax. Spotlights shone on the musicians. The walls were of whitewashed brickwork, with large photo-blowups of a bearded black man wearing a strange hat and a bleak,

97

faraway look. His mind seemed to be in some other galaxy, more challenging than the one down the street where he lived.

'Monk,' said Pat, returning to the table with the menu.

'I'm sorry?'

It was difficult to talk in competition with the music and she couldn't understand why Pat was talking to her about monks. Pat pointed at the nearest portrait and explained.

'The pictures on the wall. Thelonious Monk. Piano player.'

'Ah. Got it. Thank you. Is he a dirty bopper?'

'Sort of.'

Pat indicated the menu.

'Menu.'

Rachel nodded her thanks as Pat hurried away to the bar. The music built to a crescendo, then stopped in one last glorious explosion of chaos, sounding like equal parts Stravinsky and Bartok, seasoned with blues. Four people applauded, two remained silent, two were in love and whispering, and one man was either asleep, drunk or dead. Rachel, quickly alert to the choices, joined in the applause.

The saxophone player took a hand microphone from its stand. He was a slightly-built, dark-haired man in his forties.

'Thank you, fans, for that notable display of passionate indifference. The boys in the quartet would like me to say that they love you but not all that madly. In a few minutes, Mike Daley will be playing his next set and, by way of contrast, he will be offering you music. Meanwhile, thank you on behalf of Lenny Taylor on drums, Mark Stanley on bass, Frank Rogers on piano. My name is Paul Webster.'

Rachel thought: yes, I already know your name.

'Here, to finish our set, is your favourite and ours. Well, our favourite anyway.'

And the quartet played 'Misterioso'.

SEVEN

In a Mellotone

The quartet's version of 'Misterioso' was, to Rachel's untutored ears, a note-for-note reproduction of the record John had played, over and over again, following Ann's death. She remembered Will's comment – 'It's a Monk tune' – and realized its composer was the man whose brooding portraits hung on the walls of the club. The place was a shrine to Thelonious Monk and the band was playing the anthem; a strange, elliptical theme verging on the childlike, the work of a child who has gazed into the darkest waters without losing his innocence.

This time there was no discordant crescendo, but a dying fall that hung upon the room like a final amen. Then Paul murmured into the microphone:

' "Misterioso". And in a few minutes, Mike Daley.'

There was no applause. The corpse resurrected himself and stumbled towards the bar. The other eight members of the audience also headed for the bar, though the two lovers seemed more in need of a cheap hotel room, and quickly. The musicians made their exit through a side door leading from the stage. Rachel wondered whether jazz clubs had dressing-rooms. It seemed like an irrelevance. The musicians, though well scrubbed, were dressed as if they had originally planned to stay in, rather than go out.

Alone in the room, Rachel studied the menu. Its emphasis was on liquor. It listed a range of cocktails with names like Rhythm-A-Ning, Introspection, Straight No Chaser, Friday the 13th and Monk's Mood. Near the foot of the page, like an afterthought, she read: 'FOOD – *See Blackboard*'.

She peered through the smoky gloom, trying to see the blackboard. She found it nestling modestly between two

99

more portraits of the Master. The message was succinct and unambiguous:

FOOD
Pasta of the Day
Pizza of the Day
Vegetarian Special – Salad of the Day

It was hardly a menu to make the taste-buds rejoice, though the fact that it was neatly chalked gave it a kind of defiant integrity, like those hand-written notices alongside country roads advertising free-range eggs and sacks of potatoes. Rachel needed a little guidance on the runners and riders and looked around for Pat, the bringer of information. Instead she saw Paul walking across to her table.

'I was told a lady from the travel agency wanted to see me.'

'In a manner of speaking. But it's nothing to do with holidays.'

Paul sat down opposite her. He realized the table was empty, save for the candle in the wine bottle.

'No drink? No food? Are you not being looked after? Would you like me to sack somebody?'

'There's no need. I was plucking up the courage to order some food. What would you recommend?'

'I'd recommend eating somewhere else.'

Pat arrived at the table with a glass of lager for Paul. He looked up at her.

'Food. What do you think?'

'The pasta's interesting but dangerous. The pizza's bland but more or less harmless.'

'The salad?' asked Rachel.

'Looks very green, even in the dark. I think it's above the safety limit.'

'I'll have a pizza and a glass of lager, please.'

'Would you believe she has a degree in Mechanical Engineering?' said Paul, as he watched her go.

'Has she really?'

'No. I just made that up.'

He turned, looked at Rachel. The light from the candle dramatized the modelling of his face. She was reminded of one of the friendlier gargoyles on Lincoln Cathedral, though there was nothing stone-faced about his expression. It changed almost second by second, as if he were constantly trying on new faces, finding one to fit the mood and the occasion. One moment it was quizzical, then in turn anxious, jokey, cool, uncertain. It was a kaleidoscopic face, revolving around curiosity.

'OK, so we've established I don't owe you money, you're not booking me on a package trip to Benidorm, so what is it? You must be selling a guaranteed cure for dandruff.'

'You've got dandruff?'

'Yes, but not where it shows.'

He may be my father, thought Rachel, but he's seen too many Woody Allen films. That's assuming he is my father. Maybe this is the time to put his jauntiness to the test.

'I'm here because I think you knew my mother. She was at Leeds University. Her name was Ann. I'm talking about 1959.'

'Ann Jackson?'

'Yes. That was her name before she married.'

'And you're Ann's daughter?'

She nodded and, anticipating the next question, said: 'I was born in 1960.'

'Does that mean . . . what I think it means?'

'Yes.'

He stared at her for a long time, then took her two hands across the table, lifted them to his lips and kissed the fingers of each in turn.

'Unto me a child is born. Heavenly joy. oh boy. Bring forth the fatted calf. Wow.'

He placed her hands on the table, where he had found them.

'You certainly put a road block on the one-liners.'

'I haven't noticed too much difference so far.'

'What's your name?'

'Rachel.'

He repeated her name.

'Rachel. Rachel. You have no idea how beautiful that is.'

The knowledge carried him away into some private pool of remembrance. Now he was staring through her, but she had no way of guessing what pictures he was seeing. Then he re-entered their shared orbit.

'Listen,' he said. 'I have three hours work to do in the office, cheating the Revenue. It'll take me forty-five minutes. You sit here, have your pizza. The pizza is guaranteed by the suppliers to last forty-five minutes, assuming you have two-thirds of a full set of teeth. By an extraordinary coincidence, Mike's last set also lasts forty-five minutes, so we'll finish level. I'll meet you back here after the show and you can tell me the story of your life. Do we have a deal?'

'Only if you tell me the story of yours.'

'Do you have a strong stomach?'

'I'm going to eat the house pizza.'

He laughed. The mobility had swept back into his face, like a tide on the turn.

'Five minutes and already I love you. Madly.'

He threw in the 'madly' as a PS before dancing across the floor to the microphone. Mike Daley, the officially-designated dirty bopper, sat at the piano. He appeared in the half-light to be in his twenties. Like Paul's quartet, he was dressed for an evening at home, in a red checked shirt, the top pocket stuffed with pens and what looked like unmailed letters, and corduroy trousers which had lost contact with their creases a decade earlier. His face looked unusually healthy for its context. It had been in contact with a better class of air than was provided by the club. There was no air-conditioning here. There was nothing to condition.

'And now, music-lovers, for his final set of the evening, we have the beautiful and talented Mike Daley. Mike's appearing all week, with a variety of supports, but he expects to have his own truss back by Friday. Mike Daley.'

Paul turned and left the stage by the side door. There were five people sitting at tables and another twenty or so standing at the back of the room, anxious to maintain an immediate lifeline to the bar. They had listened to Paul's announcement in silence. Rachel decided that must be a tradition in jazz clubs. Jokes of a bleak quality were told and under no circumstances did anyone laugh. It seemed to be an article of faith.

On the positive side, they listened to Daley's piano with equal silence. There was no chatter, no clinking of glasses. Rachel was aware of hushing sounds from one or two of the listeners at the door and turned to see Pat approaching. In one hand she carried a pizza on a plate and cutlery wrapped in a serviette. In the other she carried an ice bucket containing a bottle of champagne with a glass upturned on the top.

'Compliments of the management,' she whispered, earning herself another harsh glare from a nearby *aficionado*.

'Thank you,' mouthed Rachel.

Pat timed the popping of the champagne cork to coincide with a break in the music so that it sounded like a supplement to the scutter of applause.

'*Bon appetit*,' she said, then moved through the drinkers clustered by the doorway, and into the bar. Rachel tried to eat her supper without distracting the listeners. She was the only one in the place eating. Several of the people looked as if they could use a good meal, but had given up, probably on ideological grounds. There was a lot of implied ideology in the room.

Rachel concentrated her practical efforts on slicing up a resilient pizza without scraping her knife on the plate. Once she was accustomed to the style, she timed the cutting to coincide with the noisier sections of the music. Daley's playing alternated passages of two-fisted, percussive spikiness with gentler lyrical moments. Arpeggios and glissandos tumbled over one another like kids larking about in a playground. At least, that's what she thought they were. After three glasses of champagne, she was no longer sure those were the right words, but she wanted to remember the details to tell Will. And, oh shit! She had promised to telephone Will before eleven and it was already – she looked at her watch – twenty to two. She shrugged. Might as well drink up and listen to the music.

There was violence in the music and tenderness too, often at the same time. There was no sheet music on the stand. Daley sidled from piece to piece, with hardly a pause between, oblivious to the audience. Here and there Rachel identified a fragment of a known melody. 'Night and Day' jostled briefly with 'Body and Soul' and both were then swamped by fresh themes riding in from another town. Four bars of her beloved Mahler flashed by, pursued by a stomping tune that sounded like John Philip Sousa mixed up in a street brawl with Ravel.

She was – in a word loved by her grandfather – gobsmacked. Gobsmacked and a little frightened. The music was astonishing but where did it come from? And, since it was not written down, where did it go? Was this audience of mainly middle-aged boozers worth all the effort? It was a strange club she had wandered into and she felt every inch a non-member.

Eventually, Daley stopped playing. He stood up, faced the audience, and muttered: 'Thank you very much.'

Rachel started to clap, then realized with a shock that she was on her own in the room. Daley looked at her across the empty space and smiled.

'I'm sorry,' she said, 'I didn't mean to embarrass you. I didn't see them go.'

'I've emptied bigger rooms than this in my time.'

'All the same. I . . .'

She looked around in vain for Pat or Paul. She needed more guidance, this time about after-hours protocol with strange piano players, with special reference to dirty boppers.

Daley galloped to the rescue with an explanation.

'It's Monday night. People have Job Centres to go to in the morning.'

His voice was quiet, almost withdrawm, with a sugges-tion of West Country processed by a Polytechnic. He

104

picked up one or two stray pieces of paper from the top of the piano, and stuffed them into his already running-over shirt pocket, all in a slow, desultory and drained fashion, as if his playing had used up the greater part of his mental and physical coordination. Rachel decided he needed a drink.

'Would you like some champagne? I seem to have this bottle and I can't drink it all myself.'

'Thank you.'

'I don't have a glass.'

'The management leave glasses all over the place.'

He picked up a stray glass from the bandstand, emptied some dregs of what looked like lager into someone's leftover Perrier water and walked over to Rachel's table. He poured himself some champagne, then topped up her glass. There was more grace than greed in his demeanour.

'Cheers,' he said.

'Cheers.'

He drank the champagne, then stood by the table, a little awkwardly. He obviously wanted to go home but an irrelevant courtesy told him he should not abandon a nice girl like her in a place like this.

'Nothing personal,' he said, cautiously, 'but haven't you got a home to go to?'

She reassured him. 'Oh yes, I have somewhere to go. But I'm waiting to see Paul.'

'I hope you've made an appointment.'

'He'll turn up.'

He smiled, half to himself. Rachel thought: when he smiles, when he talks, when he plays, it's mainly a dialogue with himself. Other people may join in, but it's strictly optional.

'People are waiting for Paul,' he said, 'in bars and in offices and on street corners, all over Western Europe. And once an hour, they all say . . . "he'll turn up".'

The speech was nominally addressed to her, but part of him seemed to be trying it on for size, content and tonal quality. Whatever his intentions, somebody was listening.

'I heard that, you cut-price Charlie Kunz.'

Paul was standing at the side of the stage. He doused the stage lights, switched on the house lights. Under their influence, the white walls were transformed to a stale grey, and the smoky, romantic ambience gurgled away down a hitherto concealed plughole. It was pumpkin time.

'The management gave me some champagne,' said Rachel. 'Would you like to share it?'

'What a truly wonderful and generous management it must be,' said Paul, finding another stray glass and joining the party at the table. He sat down, poured himself a drink, looked sideways at Mike and said: 'Seems like I got here in the nick of time.'

'Sorry. I need a translation,' said Mike.

'I walk in here and what do I find? Mike Daley, cheapskate piano player and pool hustler, chatting up my daughter.'

'What?'

'Mike. I'd like you to meet my long-lost daughter, Rachel.'

'Wow.'

Mike emerged fully from his private world at the revelation. Obviously Paul had never struck him as a parent, even of the long-lost brand: he was a guy who ran a club and hired piano players. That was all Mike had ever needed to know. He frowned, in concentration rather than concern.

'How long have you been lost?'

'Since before I was born until tonight,' said Rachel.

'That's really quite impressive.'

'It impresses the hell out of me,' said Paul. 'Now go home. This is a very tender moment in my life and I don't want musicians hanging around, screwing up the majesty of the occasion.'

'Sure. Fully understand.'

Mike looked around the room, favouring the bandstand, like a man convinced he had a briefcase and umbrella when he arrived, but worried he might have left them on a train. He seemed to reassure himself that he really had arrived with what he stood up in, and his attention floated back towards Rachel.

'Will I see you again?'

'I have no idea,' said Rachel.

He was happy enough with her vagueness.

'Well if I don't see you again . . . have a nice life.'

He nodded at Paul, then left, the beginnings of a frown once more troubling the space between his eyebrows. Rachel thought he was probably trying to remember where he lived.

'Are they all like that?' she asked.

'Are all who like what?'

'Jazz musicians. Do they all inhabit another galaxy? He seems to have a little trouble making contact with life as we know it, on the planet Earth.'

'Mike's a sweetheart. I guess he's got tunes going on in his head all the time. Conversation comes second. That's why he talks in quotations a lot of the time. We all do. All our best lines are nicked from Duke Ellington or Ronnie Scott. Have a nice life is Ronnie's. Love you madly is The Duke's. Music's the real way of speaking. All the rest is just filling in time between gigs.'

'There's a lot to find out.'

'For me too.'

The place suddenly seemed very quiet and real. The music had stopped in every sense, and they both understood there was a new reality to be confronted or, more precisely, a very old reality. It was easy to affect a cheerful intimacy in the half-light of a busy club, with customers hanging round and an uptempo blues bouncing off the walls. Now it was a moment of truth and they had nothing to hide behind; but what the truth was, and whether it was worth the seeking, neither of them could tell.

'There are ten thousand questions to ask you, and I don't know which one to ask first,' said Rachel.

'Let's start with the pleasantries. The small talk. How's your mother?'

It was like one of Mike's thundering discords. She

realized he didn't know. How could he? She hadn't told him.

'Oh God. I'm sorry.'

'What's wrong?'

'She's dead. She was killed in a car crash last autumn.'

Rachel saw the real face of the real man. Whatever names he had travelled under since the day of her birth, wherever he had wandered, whoever his pursuers, this was the core of his being on show, for her eyes alone. The jaunty defiance, the flip disregard of convention were set aside.

'Would you like me to tell you about it?' she said.

'Would it make any difference? You don't change the reality by adding a whole load of detail.'

He reached out, touched her hand briefly, then let go.

'I'm sorry, love,' he said, 'it must have been a lousy time for you.'

'I worked through it.'

She told him her story so far, about checking her mother's papers, and the progressive discovery of her true parentage. She even owned up to the Philip Marple fantasy, adding: 'That's nice. I've only known you a few hours and I can own up to a silly fantasy.'

'That's what jazz musicians try to do all the time. When you hit a good night, and start blowing from the roots of your being, your imagination, your soul . . . whatever you want to call it and whatever you believe in . . . when you do that, in the trade we call it owning up. That's what Mike does when he plays. It's what he doesn't do when he talks, as you noticed.'

'Will you own up to me?'

'What about?'

'About you and my mother. About . . .'

She hesitated, knowing what she wanted to say, uncertain of the apt words. He encouraged her.

'Go on. Lady Rachel. You can say anything you like to Pops.'

'More quotations?'

'Lester Young and Louis Armstrong. But this is me talking now. You've got something to say. Own up.'

'I would like to know about the circumstances of my conception. And I want to know why you disappeared.'

'And so you shall.'

They were both startled as someone walked into the room. It was Pat.

'Are you coming home tonight?' she asked Paul.

The question was not asked aggressively, but the subtext was unmistakable. It was a question asked between partners.

'Do you mind going on without me? I have to talk to Rachel for a while. We're in something of an ongoing catching-up situation.'

'It could wait until the morning,' said Rachel.

'No it couldn't,' said Paul, 'and it already is the morning, so what's the point in waiting? Talk now. Repent later.'

'Have you far to go?' asked Rachel, concerned about Pat walking home along mean and hostile streets.

'Up two flights of stairs,' said Pat.

She kissed Paul, then moved around the table and gave Rachel a friendly hug.

'See you both,' she said, and left them.

'Sorry,' said Rachel, 'I didn't realize you and Pat . . .' Again she hesitated.

'We do, but not that often. We're usually too tired. Sorry,' he added, apologetically, 'but if you leave a sentence half-finished, I tend to leap in with a cheap and unworthy laugh. It's an old weakness.'

'Do you have a lot of old weaknesses?'

'Like the great Dorothy Parker said, if they were all laid end to end, I shouldn't be at all surprised.'

'So tell me about the circumstances of my conception.'

'You're familiar with the basic method, of course?'

'Don't mess with me, Pops. Own up.'

Paul owned up, as well as he was able.

*　　*　　*

Paul Webster arrived at Leeds University in the autumn of 1958, with a Cockney accent and a flimsy academic record in school, sufficient to squeeze him into a Modern History course by a side door in a bad year. Like most of his contemporaries he was lonely and afraid, away from home for the first time, and casting around for a temporary role to cover for immaturity and inadequacy.

Some of his colleagues smoked pipes or wore bow ties or read Jack Kerouac, but in this area of self-protection Paul had an advantage. He played clarinet and saxophone. Not only could he play them, he knew several tunes.

'All these things are relative,' he explained to Rachel. 'I wasn't very good but the other musicians on campus were lousy. In the world of the lousy, the least lousy gets to be King.'

After a year, Paul was firmly established as one of the minor eccentrics around the university. He wore dark glasses and a goatee beard after the manner of Dizzy Gillespie, never attended lectures that began before noon and had a small skirmish with the authorities when he tried to proclaim Headingley Cricket Ground part of Fidel Castro's newly-created People's Republic of Cuba.

'It was a weird time. Harold Macmillan was Prime Minister, telling us all we'd never had it so good, and little baby Cliff Richard was in the charts with "Living Doll" and if I heard anyone playing it or singing it I told them: "You're a zombie and I'll never speak to you again". And I never did. Some of them were quite nice people, too. I missed them.'

Paul had his moment of glory once a fortnight, on alternate Tuesdays. The jazz club met weekly, in a room over a pub. The schools of jazz, in a state of permanent cold war, took turns. One week the Beale Street Stompers played traditional New Orleans-style music to a noisy, beer-swilling, duffel-coated audience, most of whom started shouting requests for 'When the Saints Go Marching In' after the second pint of bitter. The next week Paul Webster's Blue Notes played cool, modern jazz to an average audience of twelve people.

'To be truthful, twelve wasn't the average. Twelve was a really good night. But I always said it didn't matter. The people who came to hear us really listened. They didn't get drunk and puke all over the place. They listened to the music. I used to say to the guys in the band . . . those twelve people are our disciples and you only need twelve of those. I was a really ghastly human being. A sixty-four-thousand-carat pain in the arse.'

One night, two new prospective disciples sat in the audience. The Blue Notes, on first-name terms with all their regulars, tried to impress the newcomers by playing with additional cool, that being the equivalent, in modern jazz, of energy and verve in more conventional musical forms. Always laid back, they tried to lie back a little further. Sometimes they laid so far back they fell over.

The newcomers were Ann and Sarah, both second-year students. Ann was dark, lively, a maker of mischief; Sarah was bright but cautious. They made an ideal combination for a youthful friendship: an accelerator and a footbrake.

'That was something I noticed in her letters and photographs,' said Rachel. 'There was a kind of challenge in her eyes. She was waiting to take the world on, even if it was dangerous. She was ready to live without fear. But the woman I remember, the mother, she was different. Calm and with a still centre. It feels as if it was more of a change than just growing older. Is it because of what happened between you and her?'

At the end of the evening, as the Blue Notes were packing up their instruments and congratulating themselves on another cool and resonant blow struck in the cause of progressive music, Ann had approached Paul, with a show of wide-eyed innocence that fooled neither of them.

'Do you answer penetrating questions about your music?' she had said.

'Only if people ask them.'

'All right. I'll ask you. With respect, what the hell is it all about? Are there tunes hiding inside somewhere? Do all the pieces have different titles? I could tell the fast ones

III

from the slow ones because you played them more quickly and you seemed to play more wrong notes, through being in a hurry. Otherwise, as my father would say, I couldn't tell t'other from which.'

'If you want simple, pretty little tunes there's a shop along the road that'll sell you a copy of "Living Doll". We don't lay that kind of shlock here. It may be crap but at least it's our crap.'

'Oh come on,' Ann said, 'it wasn't all crap. That last tune was almost like a tune. What was it called?'

' "Misterioso".'

Later, he had walked her back to the hall of residence. Sarah had taken a silent hint, made an excuse about having an essay to finish and gone on ahead. The two girls would meet later for a progress report or post mortem, whichever was applicable. As they walked, he explained the tune.

' "Misterioso"? It's a piece of music. A blues, naturally, like all my best friends. Written by Thelonious Monk. Piano player, full name – Thelonious Sphere Monk. If you're a musician, you'll understand me when I say it's a blues built around walking sixths. If you're not a musician, let me offer my congratulations and tell you "Misterioso" is a tune that haunts you. Always beyond reach. Just around the corner. A sweet promise and the echo of a sad dream.'

'What a load of pretentious crap,' said Ann.

That was the moment they fell in love, or something closely resembling love and, at the age of nineteen, who knows the difference?

Rachel had listened, carefully and caringly, to Paul's account. Now, for the first time, she challenged him.

'You fell in love?'

'Oh yes. It was the sweetest moment of my life. Ever. It sounds schmaltzy as all get out, but it was like that moment in *The Wizard of Oz* when they walk out of a monochrome world into full colour.'

'I was told by a reliable authority,' said Rachel, 'that I

was not the product of love. I was the product of lust, draught bitter and sheer bloody daftness. That's what I was told.'

'I expect Sarah told you that.'

'Yes.'

'That was the cover story.'

'Huh?'

He saw the look of instant scepticism in her face and asked, with sharp concern: 'What's the matter?'

'I haven't known you very long, but I already know you're a silver-tongued bullshitter.'

'Is this a way for a daughter to speak to her father?'

'There you are! You just proved it. Listen. Tell me the truth. Own up. Whatever it is, I can cope with it. If you get it wrong, or tell me lies to make me feel better, I shall never forgive you. And that would be a shame, because I would miss you.' She smiled, unexpectedly, and added: 'Yes. I would miss you already.'

'I've never tried harder to tell the whole truth than I'm trying right now, Rachel. I only jest and dally when I'm nervous or frightened, which is a good deal of the time. And I bullshit to make people feel good. That's quite an honourable thing to do, wouldn't you say?'

'Yes. But I don't want to feel good. I want to feel complete.'

Once more he battled with a faraway truth.

'What you have to realize, Rachel, is we were both virgins, in every sense. Virginity was the norm. We all pretended differently, of course. You'd have a sticky encounter in the back row of a cinema, watching a Doris Day picture, and you'd transform it into twenty-four hours of ecstasy when you told the story to your mates. Then of course, being the cool campus musician, everyone assumed I had a hundred and fifty notches on my alto. It wasn't true but it was good for the ego if people believed that. I thought it might get us more gigs.

'That was the crazy part of the whole set-up. Ann thought I was worldly-wise, a time-served Lothario. And I thought she was, as you might say, experienced. She seemed to carry all this wisdom and excitement behind her eyes. When we were together, we both felt it was safe to be dangerous. I know that sounds bananas, but it's the best way I can express it. There was an old clown of a Field Marshal called Montgomery who won the battle of Alamein in the Second World War and he got into a bit of trouble once. In a television interview he said he'd met Chairman Mao and what a terrific bloke he was. Montgomery said: he's the sort of chap I'd go into the jungle with.

'It was like that with Ann. I'd have gone into any jungle with her. And we did.'

They made love for the first time in her room at the hostel, one afternoon. The regulations did not permit male visitors to be entertained in rooms after seven o'clock in the evening. The rules were based on a curious misunderstanding about the libido's ability to tell the time.

The experience had more in common with the back row of the Odeon than the perfumed bedchambers of great lovers. Ann and Paul reacted healthily. Instead of smoking the obligatory cigarette, they laughed.

'Is that it?' said Ann. 'Is that what the fuss is all about?'

'Yes, well, more or less, I suppose.'

They now knew what neither had previously suspected: that it was the first time for both of them. Ann giggled and said: 'I wonder if it was as big a shambles for Adam and Eve?'

'It could explain a lot.'

She then gave the whole matter long and serious consideration, before concluding: 'I think, although it was a bit of a shambles, that it could get quite addictive. I don't feel at all seduced. And I do feel we should practise. I'll probably end up giving up basket-weaving for ever.'

'And I'll sell my Meccano set.'

They knew there were tigers in the jungle but they chose to look the other way. They were healthy, full-blooded and reckless. Unwanted pregnancies were something that happened to other people. Until it happened to them.

* * *

'But you must have known the risks you were running,' said Rachel. 'I know it was a long time ago, but birth control had been invented.'

'It's no part of the defence case that we were sensible. But it is part of the defence case that we were in love.'

'So she got pregnant. What happened next?'

'I asked her to marry me.'

'Don't be so bloody daft,' Ann said. 'You know it's impossible.'

'No it isn't.'

'What's more, you know *why* it's impossible. Besides, I'm not ready to rush into a registry office and promise to love, honour and obey you for fifty years. I might go off you.'

'I *want* to marry you.'

'I doubt it,' Ann said, suddenly distant from him. Since the discovery, the easy and hectic intimacy that had informed their early days together had evaporated. She now seemed to be living apart from him, and apart from herself, judging their actions and responses on a lifelong timescale. The single act and its consequences had transformed her into a mature woman, while he remained a rootless and wavering adolescent.

'You talk to your parents and I'll talk to mine. We'll compare notes after the weekend.'

Saying it, there was a bleakness in her voice and in her eyes. There was more to confess than pregnancy.

'We'd agreed that that was the first thing we had to do . . . own up to our parents. Ann had to go home to Selby, tell her Mum and Dad she was pregnant. I had to go home to London, tell my people I'd got a girl into trouble. Mind you, she said I hadn't to say that. Her version was we had got ourselves into trouble. To be truthful, I can't remember what I said. That was the main difference. I was in a panic. She was cool and laid back, a bit like the Blue Notes, but better. She knew what she was doing. The Blue Notes always flew blind. So did I. Sorry, love, I'm rambling but it's getting early and I should really be in bed. And besides, this is the bit that hurts.'

Sensing pain, Rachel reached out and touched her father's hand. 'Tell me what happened,' she said.

'Tell me what happened,' Paul said.

He and Ann were walking in a public park. They had arranged to meet well away from the campus, at Ann's request. None of their friends knew of the relationship, let alone its consequences. Ann had become obsessive about the need for discretion and secrecy.

'This is going to hurt.'

'If I'm old enough to father a child, I'm old enough to be hurt.'

'I told my parents I was pregnant. I told them you were prepared to marry me, but I didn't want to marry you. They asked me about you. I told them everything I could think of. I made you sound a very nice person.'

'Thank you.'

'Only because you *are* a very nice person. And to be fair, they *wanted* to know about you. Everything.'

'You told them everything?'

'Yes.'

'And. . . ?'

He knew this was the bit that would hurt. He also had a very good idea why it would hurt.

'My father, whom I love and adore, listened to everything. He didn't say a word . . . just sat sucking his pipe. And at the end, when he'd heard the full story, he said: "You do whatever you think right, love. We'll stand by you. You don't have to marry the lad on our account. Besides, him being a Jew Boy. . . ." He didn't say any more. That's when I screamed at him.'

They stopped and embraced. She was close to tears, but keeping herself under tight control. Ten yards away a park keeper was clearing away soggy brown leaves. He glanced at them briefly, but courting couples were ten a penny in his trade. These two were all right. They weren't making a mess of his bandstand.

116

'Cry if you like,' said Paul.

'It's all right. I screamed it all out of my system at the weekend.'

They walked on. Ahead of them, in the children's playground, two little kids, a boy and girl, were creating mayhem by trying to climb up the slide while the noisy majority insisted on using the easy, downhill route.

'Tell me what happened to you,' said Ann.

'My mother said, "All right, so you want to break my heart, so go ahead, marry this shikseh . . ." Or words to that effect.'

'Jesus Christ!'

'Not the best phrase to use in the circumstances. Mind you, he was one of ours, too. And I believe he broke his mother's heart.'

'Let me guess. She wanted him to be a lawyer?'

They laughed. They were only nineteen, still with the capacity to heal quickly; but it was the last time they ever laughed together.

'What's a shikseh?' asked Rachel.

'A non-Jewish woman. A Gentile is a goy. The plural of goy is goyim. A young male Gentile is a shaygets. A young female Gentile is a shikseh. If you want to know more about the language, I'll sell you my copy of Leo Rosten. What am I saying? This is my daughter I'm talking to. I'll *lend* you the book.'

He spoke harshly, wearing the spikes of self-mockery like a protective shield, then immediately apologized: 'I'm sorry, love. You'll get used to it in time. Aggression followed by apologies followed by more aggression. I sometimes have to get in first with the revenge.'

'Is that part of it.'

'Part of what?'

'Being Jewish?'

'Integral.'

Rachel sat quietly, thinking: there's even more to know than I expected. I knew I would have to learn about a man and his life, but do I also have to learn about a nation and a religion? She couldn't claim, 'Some of my best friends are Jewish', because it wasn't true. She was without prejudice, but she was also without Jewish friends. Words and phrases tumbled about in her mind: chicken soup, rabbis, Woody Allen's movies, Holocaust . . .

Paul looked at his watch. It was a surprising gesture. He didn't seem a man who lived by the clock, even at four in the morning. But it had been a long night. He had given a lot of blood.

'I'll give you a lift back to your hotel,' he said, and ignored her token protest. She waited as he switched off the lights in the club, then walked with him up the concrete steps to the outside door.

'Funny, I'm always the last to leave,' he said, locking the door.

'Will Pat be all right?'

He looked up at a first-floor window. It was in darkness.

'Knitting up the ravelled sleeve of care, I daresay.'

The streets were dark, wet and deserted. It was like driving through the establishing shots of a film *noir*. The car was a six-year-old Mercedes with an impressive range of bumps and scratches. Paul explained it as mutton that didn't even bother pretending to be lamb any more. He left the dents because a good friend once told him that corrugated metal was stronger than flat metal.

'But the sound system is the best in London,' he said, sliding a casette into the player.

'No disrespect to your sound system but I'd rather talk.'

They were marooned by some traffic lights, stuck at red. Paul took his hands from the wheel and held them out, palms upward, in a gesture accepting the inevitability of his immediate fate. Rachel recognized the gesture as one of her own, and realized it had been his long before it was hers.

The lights changed.

'Go ahead. Talk. While away the long dark hours of night, what's left of them.'

'Why did you tell me about the prejudice?'

118

'Same reason I didn't climb Everest. Because it was there.'

'You said my mother had already decided she didn't want to marry you. So whatever the parents said didn't really matter. It was tacky, but irrelevant.'

'Alas and alack. It was relevant.'

Driving gently along the slow lane of the deserted Westway, he told Rachel of the slow drift towards the end of the affair that had given her life.

'We talked and talked, night after night, but we never made love again. That was a sure sign. She'd pulled away from me. Whatever road she was going to travel, she was going to do it without me. I think she knew we wouldn't have stayed the course together. Maybe I knew it too, but sure as hell I wasn't going to admit it. And the prejudice thing, that was weird. It should have forced us together. Made us haul the wagons into a circle to repel the hostile enemy. But it didn't work like that. It did actually come between us. That's how the shit operates.'

He sighed and gestured towards some graffiti on the concrete wall flanking the road. The National Front had been busy with its aerosols.

'See? They always want somebody to go home, wherever home is. Niggers, Pakis, Yids, what's the difference? As long as there's somebody to hate.'

Then he told Rachel of his very last meeting with Ann.

'We more or less stopped seeing each other. There was nothing more to be said. That's the way our world ended. With a whimper. Then . . .'

He had found Ann by accident one day. She was standing behind him in a short queue to sign a CND petition in the Students' Union. He had said: 'Hello.'

'Still the smooth talker.'

He lifted his hands in the familiar gesture of frustration and helplessness. They added their signatures to the list then went for a cup of coffee to pass the time until the nations crumbled into a peaceful posture.

'You haven't changed your mind?' he said.

'What about?'

'Marrying me!' He kept his voice down, but the intensity level was high.

She shook her head. 'You're too late, Paul. Before I went home to Selby that weekend, you might have been able to persuade me. I still think getting pregnant is the lousiest reason in the world for getting married, but I was very frightened. Ten or fifteen minutes of your silver-tongued bullshit and I might have weakened. But after what the parents said, I knew. The well was poisoned from all sides. We'd have had no chance. We'd have ended up hating each other. Even worse, we'd have ended up hating the child.'

She bit into the sturdy cream-cake she was eating with her coffee. It squirted its contents around her face but she took it in her stride. Cream-cakes had become very important to her, and she was learning how to handle them.

'And there's another reason I can't marry you,' she added, as Paul passed his handkerchief.

'What's that?'

'I have now met my future husband.'

They parted company outside the women's lavatories. He had a rehearsal with the Blue Notes. She had an urgent need. Aware of the world passing by, they nodded farewell in a calculatedly offhand style.

'Take care of yourself,' said Ann.

'Stay cool,' said Paul.

Later in the day, Sarah cross-examined her about the meeting.

'Did I see you talking to you-know-who in the coffee bar?'

'Shouldn't that be you-know-*whom*?'

'What did you talk about?'

Ann put her forefinger to her lips, looked first one way, then the other to check no one was listening, then confided in her best friend: 'Misterioso.'

* * *

He dropped Rachel at the hotel, getting out of the car and opening the door for her with an exaggerated grace.

'Thank you, father,' she said.

'Don't mistake it for good manners. You can only open this door from the outside. It was in a dispute with a Securicor van.'

He walked her across to the swing doors leading into the lobby. In the doorway he kissed her on each cheek, saying: 'Shall I tell you the nicest thing about tonight?'

'Let me think. I doubt whether it was the pizza . . .'

'Your name.'

She remembered telling him her name. He had repeated it twice and said how beautiful it was.

'I've always thought it was a decent sort of name,' she said. 'If I take good care of it, it should last a lifetime.'

'Don't joke about it. I'm serious. It was my mother's name.'

'I see.'

In the far distance a police siren wailed, trying to spoil the moment, but it had no chance. Rachel said: 'One last question then I promise I'll go to bed like a good girl. Did *my* mother know that Rachel was *your* mother's name?'

'Oh yes.'

The question drifted across her mind and settled like the final leaf of a long, harsh autumn.

'It's a good Jewish name?'

'Strictly kosher.'

'It's a dumb thing to say but it occurs to me I must be half-Jewish.'

'Have you just realized?'

She had just realized it, though part of her wondered whether she had known it all along. She guessed there must be implications, but they would have to wait until tomorrow, except it already was tomorrow. Therefore the implications would have to wait until the day after, though strictly speaking the day after was the same as tomorrow. She was too tired to cope with relativity. Was Einstein Jewish? Of course he was. He must be one of the implications too.

'Stay cool,' she said to Paul, and went into the hotel. He stood outside the glazed doors, watching her all the way to the desk. He felt very protective. He was a late starter in the fatherhood trade, but keen to learn.

The lobby was deserted. She rang a bell on the desk. From a room at the back emerged her bellhop friend who had guided her towards the jazz club listings and God knows what else. She didn't even know which God.

'May I have my room key, please? Room 1006?'

'You find your jazz OK, madam?' he said, handing her the key and simultaneously looking over her shoulder and through the glass doors. In a mirror behind the desk, she could see the reflected figure of Paul, as he turned away and walked across to the Mercedes, content that his chick was securely in her nest.

'Yes, I found my jazz OK. Then I spent the rest of the night talking to my father.'

She felt uncomfortable using the word with reference to Paul, and clearly the bellhop felt her story would not stand up in court. Equally clearly, he was happy for her.

'And you have a nice time with your father?'

'Yes, thank you.'

'You like an early morning call?'

'Too late. I missed it.'

Twelve hours earlier she would have been irritated and embarrassed by a hotel porter who misinterpreted a sweet-and-sour family reunion as a night on the tiles with a middle-aged man old enough, so to speak, to be her father. Now she didn't care. More than that, she was rather pleased; it would be a good story to tell Paul, after hours at the club.

Though they had made no firm arrangements to meet again, she knew it would happen. His was not a world of firm arrangements and rigid time-keeping. It was a world of casual understandings, as precise and inevitable in their way as the chord progressions in a twelve-bar blues. Paul Webster's music had haunted the mother all her adult life; now it haunted the daughter.

Through the double-glazed window that would not

open, London's skyline was silhouetted by a red slash of dawn. Rachel climbed into bed, but lay awake. What she had learned of her mother filled her with amazement and admiration. Remembering herself at the age of nineteen — uncertain, unpredictable, careless of people's feelings, especially those closest to her — she found it almost impossible to grasp the enormity of the crisis her mother had met at the time of pregnancy, a crisis she had confronted and transcended, emerging with a strength and maturity to last her a lifetime. It must have been her solid Yorkshire breeding.

Then she thought: what about *my* breeding? I am not half as simple as I thought I was. I am half-Jewish and I can't even answer the simple question: what is a Jew? I need to know. Half of me may be rooted in the good earth of the ancient kingdom of Northumbria, but what of the other half? What other ancient and distant kingdoms are imposing their will on me? Am I an associate member of a wandering tribe, destined to travel desperately in search of green pastures? Will I have to go into the jungle and dare I go there on my own?

And when I see slogans written on walls, will they be talking about me? Am I going to be the object of their hatred? What have I done that they should hate me? They didn't hate me yesterday.

She dozed off as the London dawn began its chorus.

EIGHT

Bei Mir Bist Du Schön

In accordance with her newly-won status as a night person, albeit still a probationer, Rachel went to sleep with the dawn chorus of London's rush-hour traffic, and woke up as what passed for daylight in January was sinking away, hoping for a better deal tomorrow.

She was already a fully paid-up member of 3¾-star hotel life, less her agency concession. Without dislodging her head from the pillow she picked up the telephone, dialled room service and ordered orange juice, toast and coffee. She thought: wow, this is the life. Is it like this all the time for Joan Collins? If so, when does she write the books? Or is it her sister who writes the books? Or do they pay other people to write the books?

With the arrival of her late-afternoon breakfast, she was galvanized into action. She propped herself up with pillows so that the upper half of her body was set at damn near forty-five degrees to the horizontal. It was a formidable effort.

She waited until she had finished the orange juice, toast and coffee, shed a silent and painless tear for the days when marmalade came in glass jars and sugar in bowls, instead of little sachets and packets, and decided to attempt another telephone conversation.

She tried to ring Will at his office. She had promised that she would call him each evening, between ten and eleven. Last night she had forgotten. She felt guilty, but not as guilty as she would have expected. That in its turn made her feel guilty. Wasn't guilt a well-known Jewish characteristic? Was she fated to go through life feeling half-guilty? These sentiments garbled through her mind as she waited for the Telecom clicks and buzzes to settle into a ringing tone and then, with luck, a human voice. It worked. She heard Janet, the office secretary, at the other end. They had never met but were good friends on the telephone.

'Hello, Janet, is Will there?'

'Sorry, love. He's out doing a survey, then he's going straight home. He won't be in until the morning now.'

'What sort of survey? Indoors or outdoors?'

'Outdoors. Some field near Goole.'

'What's the weather like?'

'Bloody awful.'

Poor Will. Every so often an architect's lot involved measuring muddy fields in mid-winter. In time the fields would be filled with cosy dwellings, or an old people's home, or a sports centre, but in the beginning was the slime. Rich, all-powerful architects employed assistants to do this drudgery for them, so they could save their rich, all-powerful minds for battling with concepts and higher aesthetics. Will was neither rich nor all-powerful. He thought that kind of thing was dumb.

'Can I give him a message, love?' asked Janet, 'he'll be here in the morning.'

'No. I'll ring him at home tonight.'

'Yes. I think he'd like that.'

Even at the officially measured distance of 212 miles, on STD, Rachel could spot an innuendo, though it was delivered without malice.

'Is that what he said?'

'You know Will better than I do. He never says anything straight out. But I think he'd like you to ring.'

'I don't want to be boring about it, but I thought that was what I was doing right now. Ringing him.'

Rachel could sense the antennae preening at the other end.

'Well if you don't manage to ring him tonight, I'll tell him in the morning that you phoned at five o'clock this afternoon.'

'Thank you, Jan.'

There was no excuse for feeling irritated, but that was how she felt. Why should he complain about the lack of a telephone call, even though, as Janet had said, he hadn't actually complained outright? That was his way. He could convey upset with the raising of one eyebrow. Besides, he had the telephone number of the hotel. *He* could have telephoned *her* at ten o'clock last night. She was out, of course, but there was a pretty green light at the bedside that lit up if there was a message waiting at the desk. It would be a warming experience to see the little green light ablaze with the implied message: somebody out there loves you.

A little later, and at her own chosen speed, she took a lingering bath, and talked quietly to herself. That was another discovery she had made about 3¾-star hotel life. You were soundly insulated against the world, you could talk to yourself and no one was likely to walk in on you with a funny look. The DO NOT DISTURB sign was in five languages and you were not disturbed in any of them.

'I like this,' she told herself. 'I like having my very own cell. Is it monasticism? It must be very close. Can a woman lead a monastic existence? Or is there another word? Nunastic? Conventastic? Sounds like a patent draught excluder. I must ring Will tonight. I'll order a late evening early morning call so I don't forget. Mind you, I did try to ring him at five. I should have tried twice. Two fives are ten.'

She had made plans for the evening. As she dressed, she smiled, recalling her first-ever boyfriend. He had taken her home from a school disco when they were in the Fifth Form, attempted a brief fumble under her anorak without, it seemed to her, any clear sense of direction, and had been rebuffed. He had resurfaced briefly five years later when, as a student at one of the dafter Oxbridge colleges, he had attempted a single-handed revival of the flower-power movement, at a time when even San Francisco was wholly switched on to gay vegetarianism. His new gospel, according to what he told Rachel, was 'Go with the earth beat, man.' His sense of direction had not improved and she had told him where to go with his earth beat.

Tonight, she realized, she was going with the earth beat.

'I do take advice,' she assured herself. 'I'm just a bit slow on the uptake.'

Within the limits of her travelling wardrobe, she had dressed in the style of the regulars at the Club Misterioso: classy jeans, a loose woollen top and a pair of Art Nouveau Revival ear-rings, a present from Will.

'Must ring him at ten,' she said to herself in the lift, then recognized she was in an air-lock leading to a public space. She must stop talking to herself, and start talking to other people.

In the coffee-shop downstairs she ate a plain omelette with a side salad, felt virtuous, then screwed up the virtue and the diet with a flying buttress of chocolate fudge cake and cream.

Then she went with the earth beat, and a little help from public transport, to the Club Misterioso. It was eight o'clock in the evening and, though the door was open, the place was deserted. It felt like the first twenty minutes of a Beckett play.

'Anybody at home? Shop!' she called, tapping on the bar counter.

'Stay cool.'

Pat's voice came from a store-room behind the bar. She emerged minutes later, carrying a crate of bottled lager, with little sign of strain. Living with Paul must make a woman strong, thought Rachel.

'Sorry, sweetheart, I didn't know it was you. Would you like a drink?'

'Yes please, I would, providing it isn't on the house.'

'I don't see why you should pay. Your old man runs the joint.'

'I'll have a vodka-and-tonic, and something for yourself, and I'm paying,' said Rachel, firmly. 'I'm in regular work.'

While Pat was fixing the drinks, Rachel sat on a high stool, leaned her elbows on the counter, and pondered aloud. It was one of the great pondering positions in the history of European thought. Perception flowed from the elbows upwards.

'I was thinking how funny it would be if my long-lost

father turned out to be an eccentric millionaire.'

'I don't think there's a hell of a lot of danger,' said Pat. 'That's why I suggested drinks on the house. Your best chance is to drink the inheritance here and now.'

But she took the money and gave Rachel her change.

'Where is my beloved Daddy?'

'Out. That's as much as I ever know. Probably picking up some of the musos.'

'Musos? Musicians?'

'They sometimes need a little reminder of where they're playing, like the boss on the doorstep saying: you're on in ten minutes. Ten minutes! Jesus, is that the time?'

Pat started washing the previous night's glasses and ashtrays. It was not a pretty task.

'Does anybody else work here?' said Rachel.

'Yes, there's a couple of part-time bar staff and a phoney chef. They should be along . . .' she looked at her watch, '. . . twenty-five minutes ago.'

'May I help?'

'The boss's daughter? I see no reason why you should lift a finger. It's disgusting and outrageous. And yes please.'

'What would you like me to do?'

Pat handed her a damp cloth, and a pile of clean ashtrays.

'Club-room. Wipe down the tables. Clean ashtrays on each. Check there's no gunge on any of the chairs. See if any of the candles need replacing.'

'Do I light the candles?'

'Certainly not. We only light a candle when a customer is sitting at the table. Paul's a great believer in false economy.'

She had almost finished carrying out Pat's orders when Paul walked into the room. He saw her and called out: 'A vision of loveliness!'

'I try to keep the place nice,' she said.

'Not the room. You.'

He hurried across to her, kissed her on both cheeks and gave her a big hug.

128

'Did you sleep well?'

'Yes. All day. I dreamed as well.'

'About me?'

'About things you said.'

The first customers were drifting into the room. Three candles were lit. A guitar player was on the stand, tuning his instrument with the infinite patience and precision of his breed. He would be ready to play, it seemed, early in April. Rachel lowered her voice, saying: 'I dreamed about being half-Jewish.'

'Oy vay! You'd better step into the office so we can talk this thing through.'

'Aren't you playing tonight?'

'No. We were depping last night. I'd booked a free-form tenor player and his daughter Kitty, but he trapped his favourite finger in the freezer cabinet. At least, that's what he said. He'd probably been offered a better gig at more money. I only play in cases of dire emergency. Excuse me.'

Paul had an extraordinary capacity to give her his total attention while simultaneously giving equal attention to whatever was going on around him. That made two lots of total attention. Two into one didn't go, but he fitted them in somehow. He had sensed the guitar player was ready to play, and crossed the floor to the bandstand. He adjusted the stage and house lights then moved to the microphone.

'Good evening, ladies and gentlemen, and welcome to the Club Misterioso. Now, if you're sleeping comfortably, we are ready to begin. Later on we'll be hearing more from Mike Daley, who's here for the week, but first we are delighted to welcome a guitar player who's been around the scene for twenty years or more with time off for bad behaviour. He's been compared with such masters as Segovia and Django Reinhardt. Only last week a music critic wrote of him, ". . . he isn't as good as Segovia and Django Reinhardt." So let's have a display of your finest apathy for the impeccable, the inscrutable, the incurable . . . what did you say your name was?'

The guitar player, who knew the rules and had played

the game many times before, gave the question careful
consideration before answering:

'Louisa May Alcott.'

'Ladies and gentlemen, Cliff Morrison.'

The office was tucked away off a corridor that ran at the
side of the bandstand. Cliff Morrison's music flowed
gently from the small loudspeaker mounted high on the
wall. Rachel recognized the tune.

' "September Song",' she said, proud of her scholarship.

'Written by . . . ?' asked Paul, as he shuffled a heap of
box-files from the only visible chair on to the floor.

'Should I know that?'

'The great Kurt Weill, after he settled in the States. He
had to leave Germany. Exit left, pursued by Nazis. You sit
there.'

'Isn't there another chair?'

'Where would I keep it? I had to quit cigarettes because
there wasn't room for the smoke.'

He sat on a corner of a desk awash with a tidal wave of
unopened letters, trade literature and LP sleeves. A pale
brown telephone peered out like a nervous hamster.

'Are the jokes part of it?' said Rachel.

'Sorry, don't understand. Are the jokes part of what?
I've forgotten why we came here.'

'Are the jokes part of being Jewish?'

'The jokes are everything. Being Jewish is a joke. Not
being Jewish is a joke, but only to a Jew. Being alive is a
joke. Being dead is a joke, or so my agent tells me.'

'Everything's funny?'

'I didn't say everything was funny. I said everything is a
joke. That's a different matter entirely. A joke is something
you tell on the run, in case the audience catches up with
you. Listen. Two New York businessmen talking. First
businessman says: "Are you Jewish?" Second businessman
says: "If necessary." When I was a kid they sent my to a
psychiatrist. He said I had an Oedipus complex. The
woman next door said, "Oedipus-Shmoedipus, so long as
he loves his mother." She bought me two ties for my

birthday. One red tie, one blue tie. I went upstairs, put on the red tie. I came downstairs, she burst into tears and said: "So what's wrong with the blue tie?" There's a Jewish immigrant arrives in New York . . .'

Rachel interrupted: 'I think I grasp the general idea.'

He looked at her, sharp and challenging. 'So come on, tell me, what is the general idea?'

'Fear?'

'Yes, fear and the will to survive. When I was a kid in school I used to get chased all over the playground, and all the way home. I didn't understand why. I wasn't allowed to be in the Nativity Play. I didn't want the star part. That was a doll anyhow. I'd have settled for the ox or the ass. Back legs if necessary. I wasn't allowed in school assembly. I had to sit in the classroom with others of my kind and do silent reading. Our own little ghetto. I could hear the other kids singing hymns in the hall. They sounded like good songs, some of them. I wouldn't have minded joining in. But it wasn't allowed. I was a Jew boy. I was a Yid. So what do you do? You learn to fight or you learn to be funny. I mean, I don't know how funny I am, lady, but I would like to congratulate you on the admirable way you're controlling your hysteria. For my next trick I would like to juggle with my neuroses . . .'

He broke off in mid-monologue and looked up at the loudspeaker on the wall as Cliff Morrison's guitar slid deftly into another theme.

Once more she wondered at his ability to retain an awareness of external factors while apparently absorbed in an intimate confession. One ear was permanently tuned to music outside of his immediate environment.

'You hear that?'

'Yes. A pretty tune. I don't know its name and I don't know who wrote it.'

'Written by Django Reinhardt. It's called "Nuages". From the French. Django was a gypsy. Another wandering tribe. There's a lot of them about. No wonder the world's a mess. Shall I tell you where it all went wrong?'

'I doubt whether there's any way of stopping you.'

He leaned over and kissed her on the cheek. 'Rachel, Rachel, you're wonderful and I love you. Just for that I'll tell you where the world went wrong. All the people got confused over the Marx Brothers. I think Karl Marx was offering us a cosmic joke, and Groucho Marx was offering us a profoundly philosophical world view . . .'

She glanced at her watch as he continued. It was quarter past ten. She thought she had been discreet. She was wrong.

'You may laugh at what I am saying. On the other hand you may look at your watch thinking, will this ever end? Does this man ever stop talking? Why doesn't his best friend tell him he's got bad breath? Better still, why doesn't his best friend ring the emergency services?'

She laughed, battered into submission by the manic energy three feet away from her face. Immediately he applied the brakes to the runaway monologue, saying: 'That's all you have to do to stop me. Laugh. Just once. It never fails.'

'I didn't want to interrupt while you were explaining the meaning of life. But I really do have to make a telephone call.'

'Sure. Help yourself. It's there.' He indicated the nervous hamster on the desk. 'There's usually a modest cover charge but to blood relatives it's a dollar ninety-five.'

She tugged the telephone free of the surrounding debris. A photo-blow up of Charlie Parker and a copy of Ronnie Scott's house magazine slid to the floor. He read her situation with alarming accuracy.

'Is this a prospective son-in-law situation? What is he? A doctor or a lawyer?'

'An architect.'

'I'd like to meet him. I have a few thoughts on damp-proofing I'd like to share with him.'

Rachel lifted the receiver and started to dial their York number.

'Is this likely to be highly intimate and personal?' he said, with a leer and an imaginary Groucho cigar.

She smiled, shrugged, held out her hands in the fatalistic

gesture that was her major outward inheritance to date.

'In which case, I'd like to stay and listen,' said Paul, but he was picking his way towards the door as he said it.

It was a short distance but there were several obstructions in his way, and he was still in the room as Rachel said: 'Hello. It's me.'

'Tell him goodnight, sweet prince, but watch those flights of angels, you don't know where they've been,' he said, still in the Groucho role, then closed the door on her with studied and self-conscious politeness. His verbals combined with the guitar music had muffled whatever Will had said.

She spooled back to the beginning of her end of the conversation.

'Hello. It's me. Sorry about all that. I can hear properly now.'

'Are you with somebody?'

'Yes. That's to say No. He's just gone out of the room.'

'Are you going to tell me who it is?'

'Sorry. Of course, you don't know, do you? I found him. I found my father. That was him talking. But he left the room in case what we had to say was highly intimate and personal.'

'What's he like?'

Here we go, she thought: the sixty-four-thousand-carat question. What *was* he like? She tried her best.

'Well, he's small and dark. He's old enough to be my father. He plays the saxophone in an emergency. He runs a little jazz club in downtown Paddington. He insults the audience and tells bad jokes. And he'd like to meet you. He has a few thoughts on damp-proofing he'd like to share with you.'

While she was speaking, Rachel was conscious that she was not only echoing some of Paul's words, but the rhythms and cadences of his speech pattern.

There was silence at the other end.

'Are you still there?' Rachel asked.

'Yes. I'm still here. I didn't know whether you'd finished.'

133

'That's the end of the what's-my-father-like bit.'

'You were going to ring last night.'

There was a scattering of applause from the loudspeaker as Morrison finished his set, though it sounded to her like an acknowledgement that Will had asked a tricky question. It seemed to say: nice one, son.

'I couldn't ring last night. I was here.'

'But you're there tonight, and you're ringing me. Why couldn't you ring me from there last night? And where is there, anyway?'

'I'm sorry, love. I'm at the club. Paul's club. The one I told you about. But *last* night when I was here, I was still finding my way around. I didn't know there was a telephone I could use. I didn't know anything.'

'And now?'

'What do you mean . . . and now?'

'Last night you didn't know anything. Does that indicate tonight you know everything?'

She knew he was asking the questions because of his deep and affectionate concern for her well-being. His voice, as ever, was quiet and reticent, yet its very quietness conveyed a sense of cross-examination. She reacted sharply, knowing as she did so that it was unfair.

'Of course I don't know everything. But I found my father. You've got to admit, it's not a bad day's work. And he is a nice man.'

'Good. I'm pleased about that.'

'Thank you. I'm pleased you're pleased.'

Beneath the formality of the exchange, resentment and misunderstanding continued to simmer. Sod the telephone, she thought. It might be all right for booking holidays, cancelling the papers and ordering takeaway food but as sure as God made Granny Smiths, it was a barrier to communication between human beings trying to keep their love in some kind of shape. It was time to fix the fences.

'Did you have a nice day in the field?'

'How did you know I'd been in a field?'

'I phoned the office this afternoon. Jan told me you were in a field near Goole.'

Learning that she had tried to ring him, Will relaxed a little. It had been the wrong place and the wrong time, but the warmth of her intention made it all right with him.

'Thank you for asking, but it was lousy. It rained all day. It might be a field on the Ordnance Survey map but geologically speaking it's a swamp.'

'Tell me about it. I love tales of suffering.'

As Will started his tale, the murmur of voices from the speaker on the wall gave way to Paul's introductory routine for Mike Daley's first set of the evening. Rachel was curious to know whether he used the same sawn-off dialogue every night. Almost in a spirit of scientific inquiry, she tried to listen to both voices. It would be useful to find out whether, like Paul, she could cope with two conflicting realities at the same time.

She heard Will saying: 'The first thing that happened was I lost one of my wellies. It got sucked off in a kind of quicksand at the low end of the site. I was wearing my York City football socks. I think they're terminally knackered.'

She heard Paul saying: 'We'll be hearing more from Cliff later in the evening, providing somebody will stand bail. He's asked me to say you're a lovely audience and he'd like to wrap you up, take you home and feed you to the Dobermann. Meanwhile, back at the pianoforte . . .'

'And then, you're not going to believe this, but we were attacked by pigs. I was working with young Bernie, the kid who came on a government scheme and we can't get rid of him, that one. He had one end of the tape, I had the other. Hundred-foot linen tape. I was trying to reach through the hedge to the site boundary with my end but there was a resistance on the tape. Couldn't move it. I turned round and there were these pigs strung out all along it, chewing it to bits.'

'. . . we welcome back the beautiful and talented Mike Daley. Mike's appearing here all week, and we're delighted to have him because he's right up there with the great jazz piano players . . . Les Dawson, Chico Marx, Edgar Allen Poe, Rudolf Hess and Muffin the Mule. He's just finished

135

summer season at the Alhambra at Milton Keynes. He should have finished in September but he got his foot trapped under the loud pedal.'

'I told the farmer about the pigs. He said: "Affectionate little buggers, aren't they?" And he peed himself laughing. But I'm all right now. Except I miss you.'

'Ladies and Gentlemen, and let's not forget the old-age pensioners at this time of year, please put your hands together where we can all see them, and welcome the legendary . . . what did you say your name was?'

Rachel smiled to herself as Will and Paul completed their respective routines and crossed the finishing line together, more or less in a dead heat, each with a familiar coda. She had absorbed the essence, if not the fine detail, of both conversations. Through the loudspeaker, she heard Mike Daley identify himself as Emily Brontë.

'Pity about your football socks. I'll miss them,' she said to Will.

The conversation was drifting towards its close, when Mike's piano playing hit the room. Tonight he had started loud, percussive and plangent. He was saving the lyricism for afters.

'What's that?' said Will, as the vibrations reached the city of York.

'The beautiful and talented Mike Daley. He's playing here all week with a variety of supports and he's right up there with the greats . . . Louisa May Alcott, Rudolf Hess, Archie Andrews . . .'

'Have you been drinking?'

'No. I do try, but my hands shake so much. I spill most of it.'

'What?'

They traded farewell endearments though Rachel found it almost impossible to hear what Will was saying. She replaced the receiver with the impression she'd promised to ring him again the same time tomorrow and, presumably, tomorrow and tomorrow. She must ask Mike to play something quieter, like 'September Song' or 'Nuages' at the top of the set. She thought: Hey! I'm learning the names of the tunes and I'm learning the jargon too. Her closing words to Will had been: 'Stay cool', but she had not told him about Paul being Jewish. Strange.

'Is it not strange and strange?' she said to herself, half-recalling the line from an old GCE text, written by the other Will.

She got up and trampled her way to the door. The distortion of the loudspeaker was beginning to grate. It was acoustic music for people with acoustic ears, and suddenly she had need of the real thing, free of technology.

Between sets, she found Mike in the bar. It felt like an accident, a little tremor of the earth beat. He bought her a lager. She would have liked vodka but guessed he was in a low tax bracket. Playing free-range piano to twenty-five people in a room felt like one of the longer routes to fabulous wealth.

They sat at a corner table. The other side of the wall, Cliff Morrison's guitar whispered sweetly.

'You're not eating Pizza Misterioso tonight?' said Mike.

'I decided against it. Pat gave me a conducted tour of the kitchen. I saw the government health warning on the wrappers.'

She offered it as a small but acceptable jest. The initial response was nil. Then, as the silence drifted on to the edge of awkwardness, he made a sound partway between a subdued laugh and an extrovert smile.

'Thank you,' she said. 'A little late but very welcome.'

It felt like the sort of remark Paul would have made. Mike seemed puzzled.

'I'm sorry?'

It was not an apology but a request for help. It had been a brief conversation but he was already lost in its logic.

'I made a small joke. You laughed. Eventually. I was thanking you for your generosity.'

'Got it,' he said, snapping his fingers in relief, then went on to explain: 'I wasn't actually laughing at your joke. I was laughing at Cliff.'

He inclined his head half a degree in the direction of the

137

music. Rachel listened. She couldn't recognize the theme, which in any case seemed to be buried beneath alternate layers of Tamla Motown and flamenco.

'It's very pretty,' she said, 'but it doesn't strike me as particularly funny.'

'It isn't funny. There was just one phrase that made me smile. He played an old Charlie Christian lick.'

'I need a translation. I'm one of the newer people around here. I need to know two things. What is a lick and who is or was Charlie Christian?'

He seemed relieved that they were easy questions. Rachel thought he might have trouble with a more advanced curriculum like: where do you go to buy a loaf of bread?

'A lick is a musical phrase. Usually one that started as part of a solo improvisation. Other musicians pick it up, absorb it into their own work. There are hundreds. I really need a piano to explain properly but . . .' He sang a short musical phrase. 'That's Lester Young.'

He gave several other examples drawn from Coleman Hawkins, Louis Armstrong, Miles Davis, Ben Webster and John Coltrane. Rachel had great difficulty distinguishing one lick from another but calculated it was too early in the friendship, if indeed it ever became a friendship, to make such a damaging admission.

'And Charlie Christian?' she asked, hoping the answer might be a little easier to absorb.

'Guitar player. The first of the great bop guitarists. He was in the same bag as Dizzy and Monk and Bird. One of the cats that hung around Minton's.'

It reminded her of occasions when she had asked Will about architecture or her grandfather about gardening. The answer to the most simple of questions carried within it six more questions. She knew about Monk, had a vague idea Dizzy was once on The Muppet Show, but Minton's, Bird and bop left her floundering. She ran away to hide behind a joke.

'Charlie Christian,' she said. 'Was he Jewish?'

'No. He was black.'

Mike took a long, thoughtful drink of his beer, then said: 'You're thinking of Charlie Gentile. *He* was Jewish.'

There was no prior arrangement, but after hours Rachel found herself sitting in the club-room, talking to Paul. While the club was open, he was permanently on the run, fetching and carrying for Pat and the rest of the staff, introducing the performers, insulting the customers and occasionally hiding in the office where he pretended to do his paperwork.

The final stragglers had been persuaded to leave. As they wandered into the night Paul had advised them to hurry, so as not to be too late for their hangovers. He generally referred to them as 'the last bastion of the alcoholic and the bereft'. He loved them very much.

Pat cleared the most prominent chunks of mess, then went to bed. Paul assured her he wouldn't be long. She didn't believe him, but there was no rancour, and there was real affection in her goodnight hugs and kisses for father and daughter as they sat in the half-light of the deserted club. She knew they had to catch up with a quarter of a century of arrears.

Paul talked about his family.

'It's a very ordinary story. Amazingly ordinary. The sort of story that comes ten-a-penny. But to you, my dear, nine.'

'Truly,' said Rachel. 'I can manage without the jokes.'

'Maybe you can. I can't. Not all the time. I'll try to be sensible but I can't promise. All I can do is tell you what I know. I know, for example, that my grandparents came to this country from Russia some time before the First World War. Exit left, pursued by Cossacks. I believe they sailed into Hull. That's about halfway down England, on the right-hand side. Near the sea. I guess that's a good place to have a port.'

'I'm a Yorkshire lass,' said Rachel, underlining the point with an exaggerated accent. 'I know where Hull is.'

'Of course you do. My father told me they built a special platform at the railway station to cope with the immigrants. A safe distance from the other platforms. So the foreigners could be decently segregated. Not sure who they were protecting from whom, but that's what they did. My grandparents didn't speak any English at all so God knows how they managed. I played in Hull once. I was working with a rock band under one of my other names and *I* had trouble making myself understood. It took me twenty minutes to buy a newspaper. The guy kept giving me a box of matches.'

'Meanwhile back at the family history,' said Rachel, firmly, and without a Yorkshire accent.

'Are you sure you want to listen to all this stuff?'

She nodded. Paul could tell she meant business; no jokes, no compromises, no fudging.

'As far as I can make out the old family name was Weintraub but between them having no English and the immigration guy being a Yorkshire turnip-head with no Russian, they seem to have ended up with Webster. It's a good name to live with. Do you know Ben Webster?'

'Not personally.'

'You wouldn't know him personally, on account of him being dead. He was a tenor player. Wonderful big bear of a man with a lovely tone. Like velvet. You could polish your shoes on Ben Webster's playing.'

'Pops. The agenda.'

'The agenda. My grandparents worked in various sweat-shops in the East End. It still goes on. Only the ethnic minorities change. For Jews read Asians. It's still part of the great sweep of history. That's what I did at university. Great sweeps of history. I didn't stay long enough to get the certificate but I sussed out the sweeps, oh yes. We're all in the great sweep of history, sweetheart. There ain't no sanity clause and there ain't no escape.'

'What about your parents? Were they in it too?'

'You bet. Right in it. Way past my old man's yarmulkah.'

'Little hat? Right?'

'Rachel, Rachel, I love you madly.'

Then he sat quietly for a moment, thinking about his

parents and how to crystallize their tough and demanding years into simple English, without betrayal.

'I'll stick with the headlines. My father was in the rag trade. My mother was a full-time momma. They were both members of the Communist Party.'

Rachel was taken by surprise. Her political stance had a tendency to wobble somewhere between the Cuddly Left and the *Guardian* Women's Page. She rejected outright all the cutprice Fleet Street mythology about enemies within but ancient mythologies die hard. On the rare occasions she met up-front, card-carrying tools of the Kremlin, she tended to glance downwards looking for the snow on their boots.

'Were your parents Reds under the bed?'

'No, goddammit, they weren't under any beds.'

She had never before seen Paul so totally serious. More than that, he was very close to anger.

'They were out on the streets, fighting the Fascists. All through the Thirties. They were in Cable Street the day Mosley's Blackshirts were defeated. They were telling the world about Hitler. Nobody else was doing that. My parents were. And the bastards didn't listen, not until it was too late.' He paused, then repeated: 'The bastards didn't listen.'

He relaxed and smiled, but the smile was skin-deep, strictly cosmetic and short-lived.

'The broad sweep of history. There ain't no sanity clause and there ain't no escape.'

'Am I in it too? The broad sweep of history?'

'I told you, sweetheart. There ain't no escape.'

Wednesday, and Rachel moved easily through her metropolitan routine. She arrived back at the hotel at four in the morning, enjoyed a cryptic exchange with the bellhop, fell into bed and slept until the middle of the afternoon when she took a little light breakfast in her room.

After breakfast she soaked in the bath, talking to herself as she browsed in the Gideon Bible she had found at her bedside.

'Is it Moses I should be reading about? Is he the number one guy? The Commandments were his, weren't they? Except he passed them on. God made them up and Moses passed them on. Is that why they call it Passover? Almost certainly not, I should think. Oh, hang on a minute, folks . . .'

She found the book of Exodus and read aloud: 'And God spake all these words, saying, "I am the Lord thy God, which have brought thee out of the land of Egypt, out of the house of bondage . . ."'

She recognized the Commandments immediately. They had never greatly impressed her, even in school. They were too categorical and over-emphasized the negative aspects of the business. It was all very well to be given endless lists of things thou shalt not do, but it left little room for human frailty and fun. Humanity could function far better given four and a half suggestions, a sensitive judiciary, a proper health service and a universal resolution never to hurt anyone. She went along with William Blake: everything that lives is holy. If you remembered that, and acted on it, you could invent your own commandments and suggestions as the need arose.

After her bath, she watched the television news and found it further removed than ever from her own perception of reality. Most of the reporters, preachers, pontificators and PR advisers looked like day people. They had gleaming teeth and a full set of lies. They wouldn't recognize a holy thing if it were staring them in the face, and that included listening to the blues at two in the morning in a smoky room.

She stared out of her double-glazed window and said: 'Tonight I must ask Paul about the Jews.' Then she went downstairs to the restaurant where she ate a plain omelette, green salad and a gargantuan pudding, with double cream, before heading West to the Club Misterioso.

'How different from the home life of our own dear me,' she told herself, as she walked down the familiar concrete stairs into her nocturnal pattern. Free of the domestic and working routines in York, she had run away to an anarchic, free-wheeling sub-world under a jazz stone in the big city and within a couple of days had manufactured a brand-new routine, as rigid in its way as the old one.

Wiping down the tables and replenishing the candles in the club-room, she thought: I am not in a rut, I am not in a rut, I am not in a rut. And she realized why. She could walk away from this rut any time at all. It wasn't compulsory. Besides, she was enjoying every minute of it. That might become a problem, by the weekend when she was scheduled to go home, but it was only Wednesday. Saturday was still several years hence.

She helped Pat in the kitchen and behind the bar, smiled in recognition when she heard Paul's jokes and asked Mike nicely if he could play something quiet around ten o'clock because she had a telephone call to make. At three minutes to ten, sitting in Paul's office, she was poised by the telephone as Mike started a long and bewitching version of 'Tenderly'. It was like a tinkle of tiny bells, muffled by a breeze. She found it more distracting than the riotous stomping of the previous night, but Will sounded happy enough with the conversation, happier than she was. The distance between them seemed to have grown. She felt as if she'd been away much longer than two days and nights.

After hours, Paul talked to her again. There were no jokes at all, on either side. 'What you have to think about is not a nation, or a country with territorial boundaries. Not a language or even a religion. You have to think of a consciousness, a state of mind. Everything is carried in the mind. That's how we survived, in one wilderness after another, while we were seeking the promised land.'

'Does Israel count as a promised land?'

'We hope so. But forty years is just a fleck of dust in the big scheme of things. For two thousand years we had to keep our nationhood alive inside our heads. Everything. In our heads. The language, the religion, the identity, and yes, most of all the nationhood. And we did it. Reviled, persecuted, slaughtered and still we survived. We learn to survive. We're good learners. And good teachers as well.

143

"Rabbi" means a teacher. Wherever we wandered, we looked at what we had wandered into, and said: What can we teach these people, and what can we learn from these people? Yes, we did all those things, and here we are. Amen.'

Rachel was unable to speak for some time though she was content to sit with the silence. She was face to face with a power that frightened her, but a power she knew she could draw upon, if she chose.

'Thank you for telling me all that,' she said.

'Thank you for making me say it. It's taken me since Monday to pluck up the courage. As near as I remember, it's word for word what my father told me.'

'When?'

'Over twenty years ago. Then I walked away from him and forgot all about it. I rejected the whole package. Managed very well without it. Then you reminded me. You *made* me remember. I guess that proves something about me and about him.'

'Is he still alive?'

Paul shook his head and said: 'No. He died about six years ago. I might have broken his heart but maybe that's my romantic fancy.'

'Your mother?'

'She's dead too. You're the only Rachel in the family now.'

They drove back to the hotel in silence. Before she got out, she said: 'Thank you for remembering all that.'

'It's part of your inheritance. Generation unto generation. All that . . .'

'Jazz?' she suggested.

He ignored the suggestion and continued: 'It's like any other inheritance. You don't have to spend it. It's your choice.'

'Yes. I know.'

NINE

Road Time

Rachel started a new career as a waitress on Thursday. She arrived at the club to find Pat in a medium-cool panic. Two of her regular staff had phoned in, reporting sick. She showed few signs of compassion.

'The lying sods. They're not sick. I bet they've gone to the Wembley Conference Centre.'

'You mean we're all missing a good conference?' said Paul. He was standing uncertainly on a bar stool, reaching up to replace a broken light bulb in a discreet and therefore inaccessible ceiling fitting.

'It isn't a conference. It's a rock concert. A group called the Video Nasties. John Peel says they're the cream of the post-modernist, hi-tech, punk-revival bands.'

'Which proves our kids are *not* lying sods,' said Paul, wobbling his way off the stool, with help from Rachel. 'If they've gone to listen to that kind of stuff, after all I've taught them, they really are sick.'

'Lying sods or not, I'm still short of one barman and one waitress.'

Rachel became aware of the two of them looking at her. They were smiling, with their well-practised brand of beatific bullshit. A week earlier she would have protested that she had no experience of the catering trade, was lousy at mental arithmetic and held degree status in tripping, dropping and spilling. But a week was a long time on a quest such as hers. Tonight was now and she had parked trivial fears in the cloakroom on her way in.

'There's one condition,' she said.

'Oh God, she's going to ask for wages,' said Paul, then took her by the hand, and gazed into her eyes with the close-up sincerity of an under-rehearsed actor in a bad soap opera: 'Regard this evening as your contribution to the family business, my child. Look around you. One day all this will be yours. Not just the physical fabric, but the cultural tradition *and* the accumulated liabilities.'

'It isn't about money.'

'Even so, I'm a fair-minded man. I'll pay you a pound for your night's work. Plus all you can steal. Plus all the food and drink you can manage to keep down.'

'All I want is one of those to wear,' Rachel said, freeing herself from Paul's sub-Thespian clutches and pointing at Pat's sweatshirt with the CLUB MISTERIOSO logo.

'You drive a tough bargain, but you got yourself a deal, baby,' said Paul.

An hour later Rachel was at work in the club-room, wearing her shirt with pride. It was too big for her, in the suburbs of voluminous, but, as Paul pointed out, it had been designed to fit the Pipes and Drums of the Black Watch on the occasion of a senior citizens' ceilidh night. She tucked in the surplus folds and quickly refined her opening routine for the customers scattered around the tables.

'Hello, good evening, welcome to the club. We've got hard liquor, soft liquor, or overpriced food. If you'd like something more exotic, we can give you the address of a nice little place down the road.'

Paul's quartet was playing the first set of the evening, and he overheard snatches of her dialogue. He smiled his approval with a fair simulation of paternal pride. She survived without serious tripping or spilling, until her unofficially designated ten o'clock break.

'Going to ring the old man?' said Pat, seeing her at the door of Paul's office. Rachel nodded.

She was dialling the York number as the quartet finished its set, and she replaced the receiver. Listening to Paul's announcements was part of the nightly pattern and Will wouldn't mind waiting for five minutes. He was probably watching a movie anyway. Paul's voice came over the speaker, mildly distorted.

'Thank you very much, ladies and gentlemen. On behalf of the members of my Palm Court orchestra, I would like to thank you for yet another startling exhibition of rampant apathy. We shall be back to entertain you later in the evening unless you take violent evasive action. In a few minutes, Mike Daley will be here, performing amazing feats on the pianoforte, and he might also play some pretty tunes as well. Tonight will be Mike's last appearance of the week because somebody made him a better offer. I believe they agreed to pay him some money. We're looking into this principle but I don't think it'll catch on.'

She put her fingers on to automatic pilot and they dialled York while she pondered Paul's words: 'Tonight will be Mike's last appearance of the week'. And she thought: why am I pondering these words?

Will answered the phone. 'Hello. Is that who I think it is?' he said.

'I don't know. Who do you think it is?'

'It's five past ten therefore I must be talking to the woman I love.'

'Correct. You have just won a clay pipe.'

'Wonderful. What have you been up to today?'

'Nothing much. Just been buried up to my ears in lethargy and sloth.'

'You mean to tell me you haven't been to the Tate Gallery or the Changing of the Guard or Madame Tussaud's or the Zoo or the Natural History Museum or the National Theatre?'

'No. I haven't been anywhere. Except here.'

Mike started playing. He had remembered their ten o'clock agreement. It was a quiet, lyrical piece. Rachel recognized the tune but didn't know the title. The world was full of tunes like that. You only heard them in jazz clubs and on silly television game shows.

'I hear music,' said Will. 'Are you at the club again?'

'Yes. I'm on the staff.'

'Huh?'

'I'm a waitress. Would you like the pizza of the day or the pasta of the day? If you have the pizza, there's a small prize for the customer who gets this week's anchovy. If you have the pasta, it comes with a complimentary sachet of health salts. If you have the salad, move into a strong light so you can spot the lettuce when it twitches.'

'Is that your sales talk?'

'Yes. Irresistible, right?'

'It's . . . interesting.'

There was a silence at the other end.

'What's the matter?' said Rachel.

'Hearing you talk like that. It's your voice but somehow it doesn't sound like you talking.'

He had noticed. It had taken him a day or two longer than Rachel to sense the growing distance between them. She had no idea whether it was a permanent state.

Since her arrival at the club on Monday she had changed, like a chameleon, to match her surroundings: the recycled jokes and one-liners, the self-deprecating humour, the affectionate insults and the harsh laconic attitude to what passed as the civilized world of the daylight hours. She had no way of telling whether the change was anything more than superficial and temporary. She knew nothing about the life and times of the average chameleon. Was the colour-change only skin deep? Or did it reach the heart? Or, for that matter, did it begin from the heart and work outwards? And if a chameleon hung around the same patch for long enough, did the colour change permanently? And though everybody knew the average chameleon used the device as a defence mechanism against assorted predators, suppose a chameleon found a patch where he, she or it felt safe, secure and fulfilled, what happened then? Any rational chameleon was likely to settle for that, like Tennyson's Lotos-Eaters. 'Oh rest thee, brother chameleons, we will not wander more.'

Her head was buzzing and restless, like a Lester Young solo, leaping across the bar lines.

'What do you know about chameleons?' she asked Will.

'Not a lot. They're extinct in York.'

'I'll check out the Natural History Museum. They might know.'

'Rachel.'

'What?'

'Are you still catching the same train on Saturday?'

'I'll be catching whatever train I said I'd be catching.'

She spoke more sharply then she had intended, but it was a response to the tone of his question, which was not so much a request for information as a plea for reassurance, with a hint of interrogation.

'But you'll ring me tomorrow?'

'Tomorrow and tomorrow and tomorrow.'

As she hung up, Mike launched, without warning, into a series of exultant discords that battered their way into a reading of 'Waltz of the Flowers' that would have had Tchaikovsky consulting his lawyers, had he been in the club that night.

Later, Rachel thanked him for playing the quiet tune and asked him what it was.

'"Mood Indigo". Duke Ellington. I thought everybody knew it.' He seemed surprised that she didn't know the tune's title.

Though she had assumed the colour of her surroundings sufficiently, it seemed, to disconcert Will, she still floundered when cast adrift in the sea of names, oblique terminology and esoteric references. She heard phrases like 'the Kid from Red Bank' and 'the Third Herd' and 'Paul Gonsalves at Newport in 1956' and felt like a tourist on holiday in Finland without a phrase-book. But her mother had taught her that experts love to brandish their scholarship, and if in doubt, you should ask.

Rachel asked Mike about 'Mood Indigo'.

'It's a perfect tune. Sad and pretty. Duke used to tell a story about it. He said it was about a little girl and a little boy. They're about eight years old. The little girl loves the little boy. They've never met but she just likes the way he wears his hat. He walks past her house the same time every day. Then one day he doesn't show up. "Mood Indigo" is the way the little girl feels the day the little boy doesn't show up.' He smiled, a little wryly. He smiled rarely and when he did, gave the impression he didn't expect the condition to last. 'That's what Duke said.'

'Do you believe it?'

'It's probably bullshit, but I've got nothing against bullshit, providing it's sincere and deeply felt.'

'It's a lovely story. Thank you for telling me.'

'You're welcome. Any more questions?'

'Yes. Paul said tonight is your last appearance. I thought you were here for the week?'

'I've been offered a better job. Playing a couple of gigs with an American called Ray Gardner. Brighton tomorrow night. Bristol on Saturday.'

'But you're supposed to be playing here. Doesn't Paul mind?'

'No, he doesn't mind. He knows it's a better gig. He'll book a replacement. There's no shortage of unemployed jazz musicians.'

A group of customers left the bar and walked into the club-room. Rachel caught the phrase 'something to eat' as they passed the table where she and Mike were sitting. She stood up.

'It sounds like I've got work to do.'

'OK,' said Mike.

'I shall miss my musical education between the sets.'

He murmured the invitation so quietly it was just audible. 'Come with me to Brighton.'

It was like the invitation to become a waitress. A week earlier she would have protested that she had a steady relationship with a sweet architect called Will, and been brought up to regard trips to Brighton, especially in the company of strolling players, in the same light as an invitation to afternoon tea with the Borgias. But all that was a week ago and tonight was now. She had changed colour, deeper than the skin.

'OK,' said Rachel.

Paul gave her the customary lift to the hotel. She found it absurdly difficult, owning up about the Brighton trip. It was dark in the car, but she felt certain she was blushing as she confessed: 'I won't be in the club tomorrow night. I'm going to Brighton with Mike.'

'OK,' said Paul.

Stupid to worry, she thought: how can you disturb the order of a disordered life?

'Why is it a better gig?' she asked Mike. They were sitting in his car, marooned in the Friday-night rush-hour traffic where it had congealed, in downtown Streatham. He had invited her to drive, though driving was a strictly technical description of what she was doing: moving the car forward a yard at a time, in first gear.

'It's a better gig because I'll be playing with Ray Gardner.'

'I don't want to spoil what I'm sure will be a beautiful evening, but am I supposed to know who he is?'

'Yes.'

Hello, she thought, Ray Gardner is up there in the frame with 'Mood Indigo', the Kid from Red Bank and dirty boppers: the Finland syndrome. The traffic eased and she was able to drive almost fifty yards further south, including a brief but pulsating shift into second gear. Then the congestion settled once more, like a fat cat relaxing on a silk cushion. There was going to be lots of time for education.

'Mike,' she said, 'I haven't the faintest idea who Ray Gardner is. Will you tell me about him please?'

Mike was patient and lucid. 'He's an American. Trumpet player. White. Used to play with the Herman band. He's a fascinating guy. Full of contradictions.'

'You mean he blows down the wrong end of the trumpet?'

An ambition was taking root in Rachel's mind. She wanted to make Mike laugh. Since meeting him she had provoked the occasional wry smile. Her remark produced another. She would keep trying.

'He plays cool and elegant, like an angel calling the faithful to prayer. Ask anybody in the business about Ray Gardner. They all say the same. He plays like an angel.'

'So where's the contradiction?'

'The man is an absolute bastard to work with.'

'Mike. I'm only a simple country girl. Can I go back to

square one? If the man is an absolute bastard to work with, why is it a better gig?'

'I'll be working with the bastard, but I'll be playing with the angel. I can learn from both.'

By the time they reached the M23 and the high road to Brighton, Mike had outlined the Ray Gardner story so far. He was reaching the end of a British tour. He had played a dozen dates around the country, with a trio of London-based musicians. So far he had sacked one piano player, come to blows with another, while a third had walked out into the night streets of Halifax crying loudly to the reverberate Pennine hills: 'I never want to see that son-of-a-bitch again. I'm walking to Wigan to get myself an honest job.'

Rachel had learned that the music trade, like any other, allowed itself an exaggeration quotient in the telling and retelling of tales, but as they drove along the Brighton sea-front, the bitter wind blowing off the sea felt depressingly like an omen. Again she put the question: 'Why is it a better gig?'

Mike didn't answer.

It was an old hotel, a tidal wavelength from the English Channel, not quite elegant, hinting that it might have been designed by a lesser-known brother of John Nash. The visible evidence was that the management had been seeking alternative routes to prosperity since the heyday of the Prince Regent. The latest attempt was displayed outside: 'LIVE JAZZ TONITE. RAY GARDNER (FROM USA) + TRIO 8 PM'

Rachel and Mike walked into the hotel lobby. It was deserted and dusty. Sellotaped to a grey wall was another notice, hand-painted in red in the same style as the advertising campaign outside. It said: 'JAZZ — UP THE STAIRS'.

There was a supplementary arrow pointing upwards, in case people were uncertain about the normal conventions of staircases. Rachel and Mike followed the red arrow. Upstairs they found a long thin room that betrayed every principle of Regency grace and proportion. At one end

152

was a bar. It was closed. A notice read 'DRINKS DOWN-
STAIRS', with yet another explanatory arrow.

At the other end of the room was a tiny stage with a
microphone and an upright piano. A drummer was setting
up his kit while a double-bass player unzipped his instrument case. They saw Mike and there was a touch of relief
in their reaction.

'We wondered whether you'd have second thoughts,'
said the bass player.

'Welcome to the slaughterhouse,' said the drummer.

Mike introduced Rachel to Kenny, the drummer, a
Glaswegian-in-exile with an accent like a wire brush, and
to Jack, the bass player, a large man who bulged outwards
in the middle, much like his instrument. They were both a
generation older than Mike, though they knew him well
and clearly respected his talent.

'We're all just one big happy extended Mafia,' he had
explained to Rachel on the drive from London.

Mike lifted the piano lid and sampled its wares.

'How is it?' said Kenny.

'I think most of the notes play.'

'You should travel with your own, like I do,' said Jack,
twirling his bass in the style of a player in a vintage rock-
and-roll band.

Mike pulled a chair up to the piano, sat down and
busked an absurd, ragtime version of 'We'll Gather Lilacs'.
Kenny and Jack joined in for a couple of choruses, ending
with a Colonel Bogey-style coda.

'They don't write them like that any more, thank
Christ,' said Kenny.

Their instruments set up and tuned, the three men lapsed
into a silence preceding the inevitable question from Mike.

'What's he like?'

'You tell him,' said Kenny. 'I'll get the drinks in.'

Kenny took their orders and disappeared in the direction
of the arrow, in search of alcohol. Jack gave a brief outline
of life on the road with Ray Gardner.

'His problem is he can't stand piano players. Well, that's
not so much his problem as your problem. Kenny thinks

some of his ex-wives ran away with piano players. Can't say I blame them. He drinks, he swears and he's got bad breath.'

'But otherwise he's fine?' suggested Rachel.

'What about his playing?' asked Mike.

'He plays like an angel.'

Ray Gardner arrived at twenty to eight, preceded by a strong smell of whisky. He was a short, squat man in his early sixties, with the texture and charm of a concrete block. He greeted Kenny and Jack with a quiet snarl, ignored Rachel and looked at Mike with malicious intent.

'You the piano player?'

By way of reply, Mike played four bars of Handel's *Largo*.

'I'm not convinced.'

Mike made him another offer: a sudden burst of double-tempo ragtime.

'I kill piano players. Where's the fucking bar?'

Gardner tucked his instrument case under his arm and marched off in search of the bar.

'Well? What do you think of him?' asked Kenny.

Mike gave a wry smile. 'He's a sweetheart.'

A quarter of an hour later than advertised, the local promoter who had hired the room and was contracted to pay the musicians on demand, made his announcement to an audience of thirty-one people. He was a thin, weary-looking man whose hair was receding in the face of financial catastrophe.

'Ladies and gentlemen, welcome once more to the Downbeat Club.'

Reactions flickered to and fro among the three musicians on stage. They hadn't realized this long room had a name, if only on alternate Fridays. Downbeat felt about right.

'We are very happy to welcome the Mike Daley Trio.'

There was a sputter of applause for the trio. They had agreed on the name after a debate lasting ten seconds.

'And it is my proud privilege to present, from the United

154

States of America, that wonderful trumpet player . . . Mr Ray Gardner!'

The response was more generous, but had petered out by the time Gardner made his way from the back of the room. He climbed on to the stage. He seemed a little out of breath and Rachel, sitting at a table close to the stage, wondered whether he would have the strength to blow music from the trumpet. She need not have worried.

He raised the instrument to his lips and blew a cascade of notes, tumbling like a waterfall, then climbing higher still and higher.

Rachel had been warned what to expect. Gardner's technique, perfected down the years, was to play a long introductory solo, then slide without warning into whatever tune took his fancy. He made no announcements of his intentions, either to the audience or his accompanying musicians. He insisted he couldn't do this, because he didn't know where the spirit would guide him until the horn was upon his lips. Jack and Kenny both claimed this was a straightahead lie and Gardner knew exactly what he was playing and where he was going at every point along the way; but there was no point in pricking the pretensions of a lifetime. You were liable to end up fired, hit or on the road to Wigan.

Gardner ended his pyrotechnics with a high-register trill then, without breaking the sequence of notes, gave a nod to the trio, and sidled into the opening theme of 'What Is This Thing Called Love'. Mike guessed correctly, and played the theme in precise unison. Gardner glanced at him. His look said, loud and clear: smartarse. Mike's return glance said: it takes one to know one.

That became the pattern of the evening. Gardner throwing ever more elaborate and convoluted challenges; Mike guessing right every time. Rachel suspected there were even more subtle games going on, but her ears were not sharp enough to catch them. It was something to ask Mike about later.

Towards the end of the evening, Gardner broke with his own convention. The effect of a hard night's blowing and

155

indiscreet sips from the Scotch he had concealed behind the drums were taking their toll. After playing a fast blues, he growled at Mike: 'My brain's seized up. You think of a tune.'

It was Mike's turn to play an elegant, allusive and teasing opening solo. He let the music dance this way and that, varying the key and the tempo, then skipped lightly and politely into a tune Rachel immediately recognized as 'The Kerry Dance'. He nodded at Gardner, indicating: come on in, it's lovely and warm. Gardner ignored the invitation. Instead, he sat down on a chair at the side of the stage and pretended not to listen.

Later, when the audience had left and the musicians were packing up their instruments, Gardner prowled across the stage to Mike, like the Bronx on the march.

'What the hell sort of tune was that?'

' "The Kerry Dance". It's traditional Irish,' said Mike.

'I blow jazz trumpet. I'm not a fucking bagpipe player.'

'Art Tatum used to play "The Kerry Dance". He recorded it. Los Angeles, 1945.'

It was a moment of truth; a very tiny and pedantic truth in the broad sweep of history, but of immense significance to the protagonists. Rachel saw Gardner's fists clench. Mike remained seated at the piano. Maybe something in the American's mythology told him you don't hit a man while he's sitting down; and maybe Mike, sensing this, decided he would save standing up for later. Whatever the inner turmoils, they were resolved when Gardner picked up his instrument case and growled: 'Screw you, kid.'

He turned his back on Rachel and the Mike Daley Trio and left the long thin room.

'You must have upset him,' said Kenny. 'He's left his bottle.'

Seconds later, Gardner returned, walked along the room, on to the stage, collected his bottle of whisky, still showing a couple of inches on the alcohol gauge, and departed without a word.

'Does that mean he wants you back tomorrow night?' asked Rachel.

'You bet,' said Jack. 'What you just saw was wild enthusiasm.'

'A bit over the top, if anything,' said Kenny.

Mike played a short, low-down, bluesy version of the National Anthem, and they left.

The sea was roaring and they braced themselves against the aggressive January wind as they climbed into the car.

'Do you mind if I drive?' said Mike.

'It's your car.'

They cruised along the promenade, looking for a sign reading THIS WAY OUT, and he explained: 'I like to drive home after a gig. I don't want to sound like a merchant banker, but it helps me unwind. Something like that. Soul of the artist, all that crap. But it was beautiful to have a chauffeur on the way to the main event. Thank you for being beautiful.'

It was a simple statement; a compliment from him to her, freely given without mawkishness or innuendo.

'Do you normally drive alone?'

He nodded.

'Do you live alone?'

'I share a flat. With a piano.'

She felt any further questions about the piano would be too intimate and personal. They drove in silence for a while. He was a man who wore silence easily and comfortably, like an old jacket. She was pretty sure that polite observations about the windy weather or suggestions that they listen to the wallpaper prattlings of popular radio would be as welcome as bubonic plague. Only when they were securely on the officially-designated motorway did Rachel ask the question that had been itching at the back of her head since Mike's confrontation with Ray Gardner.

'All that nonsense after the show,' she said, 'it wasn't really about "The Kerry Dance", was it?'

Without intending it, she achieved her week-long ambition. She made him laugh. It rumbled gently and cheerfully, a pleasant sound, far removed from a Falstaffian belly laugh, but then, he didn't have Fat Jack's belly.

157

'Is that funny? I didn't think it was funny.'

'Out of the mouths of babes. You say exactly the right thing, even when you don't know you're saying exactly the right thing. That's what I like about you.'

That was what she liked about *him*. He could pay her a simple tribute without an implied invitation to climb into bed with him. Even so, she had no idea what he was talking about.

'Why was it the right thing to say?'

'I'll tell you what was happening tonight. It was a battle. He was trying to cut me. I was trying to cut him.'

'Cut?'

'Another word from the *Observer's Book of Jazz Jargon*. You see, when musicians improvise together, it shouldn't really be competitive. Duke Ellington said it should be an exchange of compliments. But some guys, mostly Americans, see it more like the Gunfight at the OK Corral. I'm the toughest guy in the house. Rambo jazz. Gardner's like that. A street fighter. Gardner likes to pick fights with piano players. Musically speaking. It's called a cutting contest. I'm not a warrior. On the other hand . . .'

He shrugged and smiled at the memory of his evening.

'. . . you don't want to fight, but by Jingo if you do . . . ?' said Rachel.

'Yes. But tonight I was a dirty fighter.'

'Explain.'

'We all have our favourite musical tricks. Special phrases we go back to when we get lost in the search for ultimate beauty.'

'You mean licks. You taught me about licks.'

Again he laughed. Was that the secret? Say things he enjoyed hearing and prove she had listened during their earlier conversations? It wasn't a discovery to shift the earth on its axis, but it was worth a marginal note.

'Yes. I mean licks. I listened when Gardner was playing, picked out all his favourite licks, then played them back at him on the piano. Except I played my own tricks with them. Distorted them. Inverted them. Played them in the wrong key or in the wrong tempo. Turned them inside out and tossed them back in his face. It isn't a decent way to behave.'

'He'd have done the same to you.'

'I have an unfair advantage. He's blowing down a length of metal tubing. He can only play one note at a time. I can play ten notes at a time. I kept eight for myself and used two to insult him. You only need two fingers to insult anyone. That's a fact of life.'

It was Rachel's turn to laugh and, doing so, she thought: I don't laugh all that often myself. I'm a wry smiler, too. And what does it matter? I'm comfortable with this man's laughter, with his smiles and with his silences. Even though I have a steady relationship with a sweet architect called Will and, oh shit!

'Oh shit!' she said.

'What's wrong?'

'I forgot to ring Will.'

'I'm sorry. I would have played something quiet at ten o'clock but I got into a fight with this American guy.'

He said it in the tones of a genuine apology. She placed a reassuring hand on his arm.

'It's my fault.'

She withdrew the hand.

'Ring him in the morning. He won't mind, if he's worthy of you. And if not . . . what the hell? Not my business. Sorry.'

He seemed briefly embarrassed by his intrusion into her private life, and perhaps by her touching his arm. He ducked behind a quip. 'Where there's a Will, there's a way.'

They drove through the almost deserted streets of London's West End to Rachel's hotel in a silence less secure than it had been earlier. The ghost of a sweet architect was riding with them in the back of the car. Mike dropped her at the hotel entrance.

'Thank you,' he said.

'My pleasure.'

'Paul says you're going home tomorrow.'

'Yes. Work on Monday.'

'I've enjoyed my time with you, Rachel. Go well.'

He bowed his head, in a strange old-fashioned gesture. It was the same gesture he used to acknowledge audience applause, with proper grace and humility, yet subtly suggesting he knew he was worth it.

'You too.'

She stood under the shell concrete canopy and waved as he drove off. She watched the car until it was out of sight. Walking into the lobby she realized that the bellhop, as usual, had seen everything.

'You're early tonight,' he said, as he handed Rachel her key.

She looked at the clock on the wall behind the desk. It was five past two.

'I have to be up early tomorrow.'

'That was not your father, I think.'

Oh yes, thought Rachel, every inch a cheeky sod, this one. She decided to give him something meaty to brood on during the long hours of his night shift.

'No. Not my father. A piano player. And a street fighter. He got into a fight with an American, only this evening. He won.'

She turned and walked across to the lifts. As she pressed the Call button she was almost sure she heard the bellhop say:

'Play it again, Sam.'

But when she turned to look, he was resolutely studying the racing form in the evening paper.

She had to check out by noon. She had ordered breakfast in her room at ten. That way she had two hours to have a bath, pack a case, talk to herself a little and make a grovelling phone call to sweet William of York.

'Scarborough,' she said. 'It's the Scarborough syndrome.'

When she was ten, the family had decided to go to Scarborough for a traditional English seaside holiday. They had stayed in a boarding-house, played on the beach and dug sand castles in the mist that drifted off the North

Sea. They had gone to a summer show starring a frayed television comedian and an ageing singer who, in an earlier incarnation, had finished fourth in the Eurovision Song Contest. She had passed the week joyously, sand between her toes, congealed candy-floss beneath her fingernails and madly in love.

On the Wednesday she had met Jason, who was also ten years old. He was from Doncaster, his father was a miner and he talked funny. There was an immediate sweet symmetry to the friendship because Jason thought *she* talked funny too.

'Tha talks reet posh,' was his considered opinion, and any South Yorkshire opinion, once considered, is set for life, as if in reinforced concrete.

They built dams together, splashed each other at the edge of the sea, and rode donkeys side by side, Jason insisting he was Lester Piggott on Roberto. Rachel had no idea what he was talking about. Much of the time she couldn't understand a word he was saying; but, as Duke might have said, she just liked the way he wore his hat. On the Friday night, Rachel had cried herself to sleep thinking: I'll never see Jason again. By the following Monday she had forgotten him, more or less for ever, but the Scarborough syndrome had stayed with her.

'I don't want to pack and I don't want to go home.'

She sat untidily on the bed, nibbling a piece of toast. Her suitcase lay open, empty and accusingly, on a chair. Around the room was a mess of clothing and other essential items, most of which she hadn't needed all week. She hated packing.

'I hate packing. Be nice if I could do something else first. I could have my breakfast first. Then I could ring Will. That's two things to do before I start packing. Yes. Leave it until after *two* things. I like the sound of that.'

She had evolved a Room 1006 life-style whereby she lived as far as possible without leaving the security of the bed. Getting up and walking about was to give way to middle-class conventions. She crawled across the bed, grasping her toast in one hand, and reached out for the telephone with her other. Before her hand touched the receiver, the telephone rang, though naturally it wasn't a proper ring. It had never seen a bell in its life. It was more of a high-pitched, anaemic, electronic fart. But Rachel was surprised and delighted. She picked up the receiver.

'I have a call for you, one moment please,' said a woman's voice, buried somewhere deep and distant. Rachel wondered whether she was a tape-recording or a real human being, and if the latter, did she lead a full and contented life?

'Hello,' she replied, for want of a better idea, and listened to a series of mystical whirrs and bleeps. It sounded like a computer dating machine warming up for an indecent suggestion. Then a familiar voice said: 'Rachel?'

It was a familiar voice, though she had no idea who was speaking. It certainly wasn't Will and that eliminated one obvious contender.

'Rachel speaking.'

'It's me.'

'It may well be you but it doesn't help all that much since I'm not quite sure who you are.'

'It's Mike. Mike Daley.'

She stumbled through her reply. 'Oh. Mike. Sorry. Should have recognized your voice. Sorry. People sound different on the phone. Sorry. Good morning, how are you?'

She was disconcerted, partly through annoyance at not knowing him, partly through pleasure once she had identified him. It was like discovering the anonymous Valentine card was from the quiet, good-looking kid who once carried your satchel and not from the pudgy and spotted urchin who put dead caterpillars in your desk.

'I'm fine, thank you. And you?'

'Yes, fine. That means everybody's fine and that's fine.'

Clearly the purpose of his call was not to compare subtle shades of fineness.

'Are you still going home today?'

'Yes. I've packed my toothbrush and razor. Got my

railway ticket clutched in my little hot hand.'

'I don't want to screw up your private life but you did say you weren't due back at work till Monday and last night was very beautiful and I wondered if you'd drive me to Bristol and I'll drive back and it'll be very beautiful again. There are positively no ulterior motives.'

It came out in a rush, a carefully prepared speech spoken hurriedly to make it sound like conversation. She was reminded of Graham Wotsit, an earnest boy in the First Year Sixth, who had babbled to her one day in the playground: 'My sister got tickets for the theatre and now she can't go because her friend's got 'flu and I know it's a proper play but she says it's dead funny and would you like to come with me? She's given me the tickets so it won't cost anything.'

On that occasion she had said yes. The play had been more dead than funny. So had Graham.

Rachel played for time with four bars of protective teasing. 'Were you awake all night practising that speech?'

It may have been teasing but Mike translated it into a direct request for information. He answered simply: 'Yes. All night.'

'Wow.'

'So. What do you say?'

'If I say No . . .?'

'I go to Bristol on my own. I bleed all over the keyboard. I travel back on my own. Just another gig. But please yourself. I don't want to spoil any beautiful friendships, including ours. And like I say, there are positively no ulterior motives.'

Maybe it was the intrinsic sexiness of hotel bedrooms but Rachel half-wished for the hint of a suggestion of a whisper of an ulterior motive. There was no obligation to purchase and it was nice to have the choice. At the same time, despite the lurking eroticism of Room 1006, she felt it necessary to erect one or two token obstacles.

'I'm already due to check out of the hotel. I'll have to book for another night.'

'No point in driving across London in the middle of the

163

night. Check out. There's a place around the corner from the flat. It should be cheap. It looks cheap.'

'OK,' said Rachel. She had known from the beginning she would end by saying OK.

She hung up and rehearsed a speech for Will while dialling the York number. He answered too quickly. She hadn't finalized the script and had to fall back on normal conversation.

'Hi. It's me.'

'The voice is familiar, but I can't just put a name to it. What happened last night?'

'I was in Brighton.'

'Don't they have telephones in Brighton? Or are they extinct? Like chameleons in York?'

'Will, why are you talking about chameleons?'

'You started all the chameleon talk on Thursday night, don't you remember?'

She did, but through several glasses, darkly. She'd heard a lot of new music since Thursday.

'Listen, Will, can we forget about chameleons and concentrate on practicalities. I'm having to stay down here another night. I'll be back tomorrow.'

'What time?'

'I don't know yet. I'll telephone you.'

'From Brighton?'

'I'm not going to Brighton.'

'Wherever you're going, check they're on the Telecom network.'

Whenever Will drifted on to the edges of sarcasm, it was a sure sign he was feeling hurt. It was time for Rachel to move into her prepared speech.

'It's all very simple and above board. But it's also very complicated and I'd rather not try to explain it on the telephone. It's basically to do with my father and I'll present you with a complete factual statement on my return home.'

'Tomorrow?'

'Tomorrow.'

'But it's all simple and above board?'

'Of course it is, you idiot.'

She thought to herself: the lady doth protest too much, methinks. Damn right, and she had a feeling Will methought so too.

'OK,' he said, 'you can tell me about it tomorrow.'

By now, Rachel could recognize a successful gig when it hit her between the eyes. Two hundred people were packed into a room with an official capacity of one hundred and twenty. The organizers — a pair of campus lecturers and evangelical keepers of the jazz faith — compared pocket calculators, agreed they were playing to 166.6 recurring per cent of capacity, posted a look-out in case the fire officer showed up, and bought drinks for everyone, including Rachel and several total strangers.

The music matched the occasion. Gardner arrived five minutes before the advertised start time, spoke to nobody, scowled at his trumpet and the world, then played an opening solo of surpassing tenderness. The tune, when it arrived, was 'The Kerry Dance'. Mike smiled. During the second set, Gardner invited his piano player to state the theme on several occasions. Rachel remembered something Paul had told her about Lester Young, the legendary president of the tenor saxophone. Lester insisted that a jazz musician in full flow should do more than simply play a lot of notes: 'Lady, what's your story?' he used to ask. He called everyone 'Lady' and he expected every Lady to have a story to tell.

Ray Gardner and Mike Daley told their stories to each other and to the audience; tall stories, funny stories, sad stories, rude stories. Towards the end of the session Rachel was almost convinced that Gardner smiled. It looked like a hairline crack in the polar icecap. Then he sang a song. It was a blues and the gist of it was that Gardner was going to Chicago to see his baby there. Beyond that basic statement, it was impossible to decode the plot of the lyrics. He had a voice like a rusty hacksaw blade, no apparent memory or respect for words but an infinite capacity to scat his way out of trouble, without bothering

165

the English language unduly. Rachel couldn't tell whether he ever arrived in Chicago and found his baby, but it was an exhilarating and ebullient journey and it raised the roof.

At the end Gardner acknowledged the audience with an easy-going snarl, and muttered 'The trio' into the microphone by way of indicating a microscopic debt to his fellow-musicians. It was the first time on the tour that he had publicly recognized their existence. 'Give the bastard a year,' said Kenny, 'and he might even learn our names.'

Afterwards he spoke to Mike for the only time during the course of the evening.

'Good job I fly back to the States tomorrow. I could end up liking you, kid.'

It was a long misty drive home, a hundred miles and more along the motorway. The longest silence ran for over five miles. Rachel checked it by the signposts of the M4. Mike, as was his style, asked the awkward question: 'What did your bloke say?'

'How do you mean?'

'Your sweet William. He was expecting you home today. I don't suppose he was pleased to hear you're swanning about the West Country with a wandering minstrel.'

'I . . . just said I wouldn't be home until Sunday. I didn't go into any detail.'

'Ho hum.'

'I'll tell him everything when I get home. I hate trying to have complicated conversations on the phone.'

Mike said nothing. She recalled something she had read about television interviewing techniques when talking to the poor, the sick, the dispossessed and the bereaved. If the interviewer stopped talking, the subject became embarrassed by the silence and filled the space with additional confessions. Often it ended in tears, and tears made good television. Maybe Mike had read the same piece. Either way, she filled the space.

'He's a sweet man. I know I always say that but it describes him exactly. He's very easy to live with. We like the same kind of music, the same kind of food, we read the same sort of books. We agree about politics. We don't have rows. It's . . .'

She couldn't decide exactly what it was.

Mike suggested: 'Blissful?'

There was an ironical grace note in the way he said it. He travelled everywhere with irony and redeeming self-mockery.

'No. Not blissful. Peaceful.'

'And he's an architect?'

'Yes.'

'Is he any good?'

'I don't know.'

She had never considered the question before. Will was an architect, that's all. It was how he made his living. He sometimes brought work home and she looked at the drawings. They were neat, often technical and therefore incomprehensible. The pretty pictures, like the perspective view of the Old People's Home, were exactly that: pretty and precise, giving an accurate impression of what the finished buildings would look like. He was a dab hand at painting attractive blue skies in water-colour, deftly leaving areas of white paper to imply casual clouds sometimes with a threat of scattered showers later in the day. The job of an architect's sky, he said, was to make the building look better.

'If I was an architect,' said Mike, 'I'd start by redesigning the entire world.'

'And then you'd march into Poland?'

'Low blow,' he said, 'and not true.'

'Let me try again. You don't want to be the greatest piano player the world has ever seen. But you *do* want to be the greatest piano player Mike Daley is capable of becoming. Coasting along in fourth gear isn't fast enough. It's got to be overdrive all the time.'

'Yes. Except when I'm driving.'

'I think Will's happy to coast along.'

'It's nothing to be ashamed of. Most people do it.'

Mike seemed to draw a line across that chapter of the conversation. He accepted that most people were content to coast along, with minimal ambition. He didn't condemn them for it. He simply wrote them off. Niceness and nastiness were irrelevant. If you had talent, your job was to head for the nearest tightrope. If you had to cross it in the company of a mean-spirited bastard like Ray Gardner, it added a little spice to the trip. There was no other sensible way to live.

They were driving past Slough, and Mike was quoting John Betjeman, with approval, when Rachel changed the subject and asked him: 'Did you book me into that place?'

'What place?'

'You said there was a cheap hotel around the corner. You'd book me a room there, you said.'

'I booked you in somewhere even cheaper.'

'Like where?'

'Like my place.'

'Ho hum, Sir Jasper.'

'It seems silly paying money to stay somewhere. And it's all above board. There are two rooms. One of us will have to share, that's all.'

It tumbled out, another over-casual, carefully-prepared speech.

'Share?' said Rachel.

'With the piano.'

He expected her to accept his total freedom from ulterior motives, and she did. He played clean.

Mike lived in a basement flat in Shepherd's Bush. It was near enough to BBC Television Centre for him to scream at the Director-General about the Corporation's feeble-minded jazz policy but he had given up: the guy was irredeemably uncool.

There were two rooms, as promised: a living-room with a piano and a convertible, and a bedroom with a bed. He insisted on Rachel having the bedroom. She offered a token protest.

'I'll be all right in here,' she said.

'I changed the sheets. You're having the bed whether you like it or not.'

'I see. This has all been carefully planned.'

'I'm an exceedingly clean person. I change the sheets every Saturday. Purely in the interests of hygiene.'

He suggested hot cocoa. It was a perfect idea for the occasion. They drank their cocoa from mugs with politically-motivated slogans, ate ginger biscuits and traded silly stories about their childhood. It was like a midnight feast in the dorm, though neither of them had been within a million miles of the public-school system. They were fine advertisements for its abolition.

Rachel looked around the living-room. It was exceedingly clean and tidy.

'My Grandma would say you keep the place really nice. I thought you were a dirty bopper?'

'That's a musical reference and, in any case, I'm not. The real dirty bopper's a lovely guy called Bruce Turner. He joined the Lyttleton band in the 1950s and . . .

'Mike.'

'What?'

'I don't think there's room in my head for any more jazz history.'

'As you wish. You've done very well. It's been quite a week. I understand that. You need time for your soul to catch up.'

They talked in an idle, fragmentary way about the week: about her successful search for a father; about her newly discovered blood-line; about the existence or otherwise of half-Jewish jokes; about windy nights in Brighton and the mist over the West Country.

Then, as her eyes began to close, he said: 'That's all, folks.'

He wished her good-night at the bedroom door. She thought he was going to kiss her on the cheek, but he didn't. She was sorry about that. It was innocent beyond all belief, and therefore all the more alarming.

As she closed the bedroom door on him, she said: 'I think you're the cleanest bopper in the world.'

TEN

Back In Your Own Back Yard

The train left King's Cross at one o'clock. Mike drove her
to the station.

'There's never any traffic on a Sunday,' he said.

Sitting in the car, Rachel looked at the hundreds of
vehicles streaming in many directions and thought: if there
is no traffic, what am I looking at? Then she realized that,
in a Londoner's vocabulary, it only became traffic when it
seized solid in a homogeneous lump. Wow, she decided, I
am thinking like a Londoner: I am becoming a metropolitan sophisticate.

At the barrier, she thanked Mike.

'For what?'

'For the overnight accommodation. For the morning
coffee and toast. For the taxi ride.'

'I haven't even given you your present yet.'

'Oy vay! There's a present as well?'

He gave her a cassette. On it was hand-written: MIKE'S
GREATEST HITS.

'There are some quiet tunes on it. Useful if you have to
make phone calls.'

'Thank you,' she said, and kissed him on the cheek. He
seemed a little startled by such a gesture in a public place,
even though they were surrounded by people in assorted
farewell postures. The moment was leaning on an uncertainty, which stayed unresolved as they saw Paul and Pat
running across the concourse towards them. Paul was
brandishing a bunch of flowers.

'A floral tribute from your father. A bit over-priced but
very sincere. The only place you can buy flowers on a
Sunday is outside hospitals.'

'How did you know which train I was catching?'

'I had an anonymous phone call from a broken-down piano player called Mike Daley.'

'We'd also like you to accept these, with the compliments of the management,' said Pat, handing her a plastic carrier bag from Dobell's Jazz Record Shop.

'Not to be opened until Christmas, your birthday, or when you are on the train, whichever is the earliest,' said Paul, as Rachel peered inside the bag.

By the time she extricated herself from their presents, flowers, energy and affection, Mike had disappeared.

On the train, she looked at her presents. They were an LP by Thelonious Monk, including 'Misterioso', and two books: Duke Ellington's autobiography and *The Joys of Yiddish* by Leo Rosten. They were not new. They were old, dog-eared and much loved. The carrier bag, too, had given long and loyal service and was due an OBE though it probably didn't have the requisite breeding.

At the bottom of the bag she found a letter from Paul. It was typed on the club notepaper. She read:

Rachel, Rachel

And so, every night this week, until Friday when you ran away to sea with the buccaneering Mike Daley (he's a sweet man, by the way, and 500 times the musician I'll ever be) now where was I? I've lost the sentence. Start again . . .

That's it. Got it. Every night this week we sat down after hours and I tried to tell you the story of my life. That's to say, you *made* me. I'm much happier with the spiel and the crap, but you insist on the truth, so help me, so be it. I did try.

You must realize how traumatic this has been for me too. In the time-honoured line: you have made a happy man feel very very old. Here I am, gallantly projecting the image of a gay blade (that means jolly, carefree, devil-may-care with a touch of the Sir Percy, yes, and Harry Percy too) and then Wham! Bam! Allakkazzam! (which is a quote from an old Stan

171

Kenton/Nat Cole number though I may have got the spelling wrong) and the minute I open brackets I lose the sentence, sorry, sweetheart, start again . . .

Wham! Bam! Allakkazzam! I've got a 26-year-old daughter! That drives a horse and cart through the image. The gay blade is blunted and loses its cutting edge. I look in the mirror and see a face full of wrinkles. The eyes sunk so deep in the head they look like they belong to the bloke behind.

Why am I telling you all this?

Because just as half of me is you, the greater part of you is me. You are my sole progeny, though to be honest, you don't look much like a progeny. If this was a lousy movie, a *really* lousy movie, I could say — you are the only thing I have in the world. That's the trouble with Life. It does imitate Art but when it does it always imitates really lousy fifth-rate Art. I don't much want to be like Hamlet and definitely not Lear, but God help us, does it have to be Lassie meets Andy Hardy? Being 26 you're probably thinking: who the hell are Lassie and Andy Hardy? A clue. One of them was a dog.

Another thing I wanted to tell you . . .

I had this dream that one day I'd meet you. I'd walk into a room, you'd be there and, I'd *know*! That's my daughter. The blood instinct or some such garbage. Well, I walked into the club room when Pat told me you were there and I'd been told you wanted to see me and I looked at you and I hadn't the faintest idea who you were.

Sorry. Another romantic fallacy bites the dust.

There are other things you should know that I didn't tell you during the week, like . . .

I once went to prison. Not for very long, and under one of my other names. It was for receiving property, knowing it to be stolen. Nobody got hurt, including me, and I became the best prison librarian in the history of penal institutions.

I have lived with three women in my life.

Consecutively. Not at the same time. Pat you know. Gillian you met in the Cotswolds. Before Gillian there was a girl called Maureen who was part of the stolen property deal. There's nothing like a short prison sentence to screw up a relationship and it did. It's going to sound schmaltzy as all get out but your Mother was the only one I ever made music for and who made music for me. There. That's a cue for angel choirs and gypsy violins and roll the credits if ever I saw one.

I haven't been much of a father and you should be grateful I'm not all you've got. Your guy Will sounds like a good cat, and John alias your Dad, so to speak, obviously made a fine job of being your father. I wish it had been me though I don't think I would have been very good at it. Mind you, it's impossible to tell. I might have been remarkable at taking you to the park to feed the ducks. But isn't that a daytime activity? I don't get along too well with sunlight.

Trouble is, we'll never know. That's a hell of a pain to live with. Not knowing. I might have been the Greatest Father since whoever it was that was the Greatest Father. I hope this doesn't turn out to be my tragedy. I'll smile and whistle under all difficulties and try not to let it happen.

I enjoyed our time together more than you can possibly understand. I was very angry (*nicely* angry) when Mike stole you away from me. I had more confessions and more wisdom to pass on. As it is, you'll have to manage with what I managed to say in the time available, and in this letter. I don't know whether any of it matters a damn. There's a lovely poem by Christina Rossetti (Dig that! The man has an intellect!) called 'When I Am Dead' (who's gonna buy a poem with a title like that?) and there's a little repeating theme in it, like a bluesy lick, that runs:

And if thou wilt, remember.
And if thou wilt, forget.

Meaning take it or leave it, baby. Forget everything I told you *but*, if you choose to remember anything, remember all that stuff my father told me, which I told you. Don't run away from the Jewish thing. Embrace it. It's deadly but beautiful. So what else is worth embracing?

Love you madly

Paul

PS My grandfather used to call my mother (who was Rachel, as you know) by a pet Yiddish name. As such it's impossible to spell (Rosten will explain why) but it probably looks something like ZIGAINEKE. It means Little Gypsy. When I'm much older and even more boring, that's what I'll call you. You should make determined efforts to stop me. LYM.

After reading such a letter, there was little Rachel could do but stare out of the window and watch middle England staring back: Peterborough, Grantham, Retford and between them large, brown, hedgeless cost-effective fields. Another journey: travelling again, but was she travelling hopefully or desperately? She had heard a story once, told by a Tyneside playwright called Tom Hadaway in a television interview. There was an African tribe which provided bearers for Empire-building British explorers during the last century. After walking twenty miles or more, carrying the white man's burden, the Africans stopped and sat down. The white men, eager to extend Her Gracious Majesty's frontiers even further before nightfall, were perplexed and irate.

'Why have you stopped walking?'

The explanation was: 'After walking so far, we must wait until our souls catch up.'

Rachel had travelled many miles during her week in London. Now she needed time for her soul to catch up.

Will was at the barrier to meet her. He took her case, and the flowers, then contrived a kiss and a hampered hug.

'I've missed you,' he said.

According to all the scripts, she should have said, 'I

missed you, too', but what she said was: 'Thank you.'

In the car, he asked her: 'Are you going to tell me about him?'

'Who?'

'Your long-lost father. Who do you think?'

'Sorry. I met an awful lot of people this week. I need time for my soul to catch up.'

She glanced across at him. The beginning of a frown was scratching the space between his eyebrows. He had asked about Paul, but her careless response had indicated there was someone else as well. In a way, there was, but she felt no guilt about Mike. Why should she? The sum of their relationship consisted of a couple of motorway trips, much jazz talk punctuated by easy silences, one night of scrupulous chastity, a gift of music and a peck on the cheek at King's Cross station. It was hardly in the Antony and Cleopatra league: not a barge or a burnished throne in sight. Sins were bad enough, but self-righteous innocence – that was *really* deadly.

Will had prepared his special baked pasta, with a side salad and a bottle of their cheap and cheerful house red. It was lovingly and impeccably presented. It was also totally predictable. Leaving the train at York and seeing him at the barrier she had thought: there's a sweet man who's going to surprise me with baked pasta, side salad and house red.

Fortunately, she was hungry and she was able to attack the meal with an enthusiasm that concealed the emotional ripples. She gave Will a full, chronological account of her week in London. The news that she was half-Jewish coincided with her second glass of wine. Will's response was invisible to the naked eye.

'So?'

'I'm half-Jewish. Isn't that worthy of comment?'

'I'm not prejudiced.'

'I know that. You're the most tolerant man in the world.'

'Thank you. Tell me some more.'

She poured herself a third glass of wine and told him

about Mike. It was what the politicos call a full and frank account, but unlike them, she told the truth and nothing but the truth, chastity and all.

When she had finished, Will smiled and said: 'Good. I knew I was silly to get worried.'

'What were you worried about?'

'When I spoke to you on the phone, I said you sounded like a different person. I suppose I was imagining all sorts of things going on.'

'Like . . . infidelity?'

He shrugged and said nothing but his silence acknowledged the point. He *had* been worried about infidelity. He reached out and touched her hand.

'I'm sorry, love,' he said. 'I apologize. I know you better than that.'

He was certain that he knew her. His certainty rankled. During the past week she had made shattering discoveries about herself. At one end of the time-scale was a national and cultural inheritance stretching back to the Old Testament and beyond; at the other end, she had found a taste for sudden, impulsive decisions. She had turned her daily ritual inside out and become a night person with no trouble at all. Perhaps it was all an illusion of living life on a tightrope, but it felt different. At the very least, there were huge areas of uncertainty within herself, still to be resolved.

She was churned up inside with teeming contradictions. In many ways it was a good feeling. It was sharp and bracing. Maybe at the end of it, the waves would settle, and she would resume her previous tranquil pattern. But here and now she was in a turmoil, and for Will to assume, with his familiar, cool tolerance, that he knew her was nonsense. She knew sod all about herself, so how could he know *anything*?

For the first time in the peaceful years of their loving friendship, she felt a need to annoy him, and perhaps even, hurt him. She wanted to push him nearer to the precipice, and reveal his fear, his passion, his rage. Perhaps he had none. If so, she had to know.

Over coffee, she asked the question, aware of how flabby and feeble it sounded.

'Will. Tell me about being an architect.'

'Sorry, miss. Don't understand the question.'

'How good are you at being an architect?'

'Good enough to make a reasonable living. I'll never be rich and famous. They'll never do a South Bank Show about me.'

'That's not what I mean.'

She frowned, trying to work out exactly what she did mean. She owned up about the origin of the question.

'It was something Mike asked me about you. He wanted to know how good an architect you were. I said I didn't know. We'd never talked about it. The thing is, Mike wants to be the greatest piano player that he, Mike Daley, is capable of becoming. So the question is, do *you* want to become the greatest architect you are capable of becoming? Would you walk a tightrope across a canyon, every night of the week, to achieve it? Now do you understand the question?'

She had already told Will about the triumphant nightmare of Mike's gigs with the monstrous Ray Gardner, and now he understood the question, and its underlying challenge.

'It might come as a great disappointment to you, but I know my limitations. As an architect, I'm Second Division. Good Second Division, but that's my class. I accept it. We can only work within our own limitations.'

'You can try to set new limits.'

'Priorities. Life comes first. Work comes second. I'm not going to bleed all over the drawing-board. It isn't my style.'

'That's all right. Bleeding isn't compulsory.'

They cleared the table, washed up, then settled in armchairs to finish the second bottle of wine. It had, inevitably, been a two-bottle meal.

'He must be a hell of a piano player,' said Will. It was the first time he had mentioned Mike since the conversation at the table.

'Would you like to hear a tape?'

'Yes please.'

Though as Rachel put the tape on the machine, she reflected: maybe he's thinking No thank you, the last thing I want to hear is that trouble-making, cheapskate piano player who preaches at me about Art at a safe distance. But he would never say so. Was that their problem? At what point did a conspiracy of silence become deafening?

Rachel sat down and music filled the room. It had been recorded at Paul's club on the equipment she had seen lying around backstage. In any case, she would have recognized the background murmuring from the bar, the familiar rattle of glasses and the sudden cry from Pat followed by a crash of a falling tray; but dominating everything was the piano.

He played 'Mood Indigo' and 'Tenderly' and an original piece of his own which he called: 'Stomping March for Limping Men in two minor keys and one major'. Such a title, he argued, would guarantee his staying well clear of the Top Twenty, commercial success and the inevitable corruption that followed.

At the end of the piece, there was an abrupt silence, cutting into the middle of the audience applause. Rachel got up, assuming it was the end of the tape. Then they heard Mike's voice: 'Just one more. This is for you, Rachel. Paul says it's a tune you like. I'll have to play it quietly so as not to disturb the neighbours. You can play this one when it's time to ring your bloke.'

He played 'Misterioso'. As he promised, it was quiet, tactful and sensitive, an impeccable composition of notes floating elegantly in space.

She looked at Will, but he was leaning back in his chair, staring at the ceiling. He must have been aware that Mike was treading the tightrope specially for her. It may not have been infidelity, in strict legalistic terms, but sure as hell it was the next worst thing.

Monday morning arrived like a secret signal telling the world: normal service will now be resumed. All around her the city of York informed Rachel that nothing had changed. A little snow fell, there was a rapid thaw and people paddled through the slush to book their summer holidays with Glenn Travel. Joan cursed at recalcitrant customers and the VAT-man behind their backs. Dawn called at the flat on Wednesday night, after a dismal evening at a local disco, to make sure Rachel and Will were coming to lunch the following Sunday.

'I need you,' she said to Rachel, 'even if you're only half a sister.'

'Don't you want to hear about your new uncle? Or whatever he is?'

'Save it till Sunday. Everything went wrong at the disco and I've got a broken heart. It'll be better by the weekend.'

'Why don't we invite grandparents?' said Will.

'No,' said Rachel, 'I want to keep them for a special occasion.'

'Have you got any idea what the woman's talking about?' Dawn asked Will.

'No.'

On Sunday, tradition reasserted itself, smoothly and without comment. John and Will sat in the living-room, discussing the previous day's soccer results, while Rachel and Dawn prepared lunch in the kitchen.

'I've been thinking about what you said the other night,' said Dawn. 'I make it your long-lost Daddy is my illegitimate time-warped stepfather. Does he strike you as warped in any way?'

'See what you think.'

She handed Dawn a postcard. It had arrived at the flat the previous morning. The picture was a 1940 portrait of the great Billie Holiday, with flowers in her hair.

'Read it,' said Rachel.

Dawn read the message. It said:

Paul's Jazz Stories No. 743
Joe Venuti, violinist, used to send Wingy Manone, one-armed trumpet player, a single cuff-link every Christmas. LYM, Paul.
PS Read Bernard Malamud.

Dawn returned the postcard, saying: 'I think I could get to like the man.'

'I think so too. You realize he's Jewish?'

'What does that mean? You have to shave your head? Oh no, it isn't that, you've got to give up bacon butties. That's awful. I can't imagine a civilized life without bacon butties.'

'It won't be necessary. And I'm learning a lot of really fabulous jokes.'

'Name one.'

'OK. Try this. Two rabbis talking. First rabbi says, "Life is like a fish." The second rabbi says: "That's the craziest thing I ever heard." The first rabbi says: "All right. So life *isn't* like a fish".'

Dawn gave the joke serious thought. She was a keen student of jokes, and they were not to be taken in a light-hearted way, especially when she was treading in the shallow end of a new genre. She concluded, without a trace of a smile:

'I think I could get to like the man. I think I could even get to like the jokes. And, of course, I've liked you all the time.' She gave Rachel a hug, then added: 'I hope you've sent *him* a postcard.'

'Written but not posted.'

She showed Dawn the card. The picture was of York Minster. The message read:

> *Rachel's Yorkshire Folklore*
> Two Yorkshiremen talking after seeing Bob Hope at the Palladium. 1st Yorkshireman: What do you reckon? 2nd Yorkshireman: Not bad, if you like laughing. Love you filially, R.'

'Wonderful,' said Dawn, giving her sister another big hug, 'and welcome back to the family.'

'I never left,' said Rachel.

'I'm told we all leave in the end.'

Rachel realized her sister had grown up rapidly in the months since their mother's death. She had been forced to accept adult responsibility and, after the first agonizing days, had begun to enjoy it. Forced along the tightrope, she had reached the other side, strong and assured.

Lunch was a cheerful occasion and almost like old times except, by definition, the old times had gone and would never return. John was relaxed and amused them with the week's tales out of school. The themes were constant: saintliness in the staffroom, protection rackets in the playground, lunacy in the local bureaucracy and wackiness in Whitehall. Only the names changed.

When coffee was finished, John stood up and turned to Rachel. 'If you'd like to step into the greenhouse, I think it's time we had some grown-up talk.'

During the meal, Rachel had talked in vague, general terms about London: about the traffic, the bellhop at the hotel, the bags of garbage on every street corner. The family had a proper, open-minded, Yorkshire prejudice against London. The whole nation was going to hell at high speed, and the capital was leading the way. That was what capitals were for. You only had to look at Ancient Rome.

Once in the greenhouse, the tone of the conversation changed. There were no more cute remarks about North and South. They had a more vital agenda, and John, to her relief, met it head-on.

'You found him?'

'Yes.'

'Did you like what you found?'

'Yes.'

'Rachel. I think you should know that I'm very much better now. It'll sound silly when I tell you about it, but I'll tell you anyway. I was leaving school one afternoon, while you were away, walking across the playground to the car. And it was as if a cloud lifted from above my head. I could hear your Mum's voice saying: "It's all right – better now." Like she used to say to you when you'd not been well. Is that silly?'

'No. That's marvellous.'

'I still miss her. I still cry sometimes. But I'm living again. I think I'm easier to live with. Ask Dawn.'

'I didn't ask her. She told me.'

'And you're looking very much better. I don't know what happened in London, but it was obviously good for you.'

It was more than routine politeness. He had looked hard into her face, seen the difference and reported it. Nobody else had said it – not Will, nor Dawn, nor Joan.

'Thanks, Dad.'

He shuffled, trying to find a little more comfort on the old rabbit hutch. It was not designed for sitting on. It was designed for rabbits.

'I suppose what I was trying to say, with all that about the clouds lifting, is this. I am very much stronger now. If you want to tell me who he is, I'm sure your mother wouldn't mind my knowing. And I would like to know, because it would help me to know you better.'

'You're sure?'

'Quite sure.'

'All right. His name's Paul Webster. He was a History student but he didn't finish the course. He played saxophone and had a band called the Blue Notes.'

'Paul Webster!'

'Did you know him?'

'Oh yes. Not all that well. We'd meet in the bar, that kind of thing. Paul Webster. Oh yes. Nice man. Funny and lively. Lots of energy. That's what I remember. Almost too much energy. Too much for me, certainly. I've never been one for hyperactivity. Relaxation's much more attractive.'

He stood up. 'My bottom's killing me. Let's take a turn around the garden. Check for poachers.'

Walking round the garden, John put his arms around her shoulder, and asked: 'Do you feel yourself changing? It's bound to make a difference.'

'Yes. But I'm still not sure *how* I'll change.'

'Just relax and let it happen. It was only after my parents died that they had any real influence on me. That was when I had time to think about them. About their talents and their values, yes, and their frustrations and failures, too. Very like you and your Mum. Death makes you stand aside and examine someone's life. With a bit of luck you can learn from it. Mind you, it's different with Paul. You can learn from a mature, living person.'

'I'm not sure about mature.'

'All the better. He's still growing. You're still growing. You can learn from each other.'

'Yes. We're learning jokes from each other. Yorkshire jokes and Jewish jokes. Did you know he was Jewish?'

'I didn't know that.'

Then John realized the implication of what she had said.

'That's very exciting. You're part of a tradition, do you realize that? All those artists and writers and scientists and philosophers . . .'

'And jazz musicians and stand-up comedians,' Rachel added.

'Compare it with being pure Yorkshire. What can Yorkshire offer by comparison? Cricketers. Not much else.'

'Henry Moore and J. B. Priestley?'

'They're from Bradford. Bradford's different from Yorkshire. It seceded just before the First World War.'

'What about Yorkshire comedians?'

He nodded, accepting the point, but found an immediate counter. 'There *are* Yorkshire comedians, but they don't like being laughed at. It spoils everything. What Yorkshiremen really like is gloom. So they can moan about it.' Again he squeezed her shoulder. 'You've done well with your choice of father. I wish you joy of him.'

Rachel was moved and astonished by John's behaviour. The silly, giggly conversations were a family institution she remembered from childhood, when she and John would improvise surrealistic fairy stories wherein Snow White and Mr Toad shared bizarre adventures on beanstalks with Ella and Louis, the pet rabbits, and Chico, the fabled tortoise. Other leading players usually included Mrs Gallagher, who ran the day nursery, Mr Cooper from the corner shop, and Rachel and Dawn, two beautiful little girls with wicked and cruel parents. They were terrific

183

stories, and much better than those you saw on television or bought from shops.

The text had changed but the spirit was constant and, Rachel now realized, indestructible. She also wondered whether her insistence on finding her natural father had, in some way, helped John in his healing process. Despite the scepticism and opposition on all sides, she had set out along the valley, not knowing what shadows lay in wait. Perhaps her example had helped him on the long journey through his own valley of the shades.

Dawn and Will watched them through the living-room window. They saw two people, strolling arm in arm, as in an English country garden, talking and laughing, easy in the cold afternoon.

'That's a bit worrying,' said Dawn. 'They look happy. What do you think they're talking about? Us?'

'No. Pound to a penny, they're talking about life.'

'Life. That old thing. I'm told it's like a fish.'

Wednesday was early closing day at Glenn Travel. Joan was going to play squash. It was her latest enthusiasm.

'The theory is you lose weight and it's good for you.'

'And?' said Rachel, realizing there was more to it than that.

'You *do* lose weight, galloping about the court, trying to find the bloody ball. You end up knackered and sweaty. You lose a few pounds. You go to the bar and booze it all back again.'

'Why do you do it?'

'I bought this track-suit in the sales. Don't go away.'

Minutes later, Joan emerged from the small back room, wearing the track-suit. It was a rich purple, with white flashes on the arms and legs, and a mystical badge on the jacket. Joan mimed a couple of impressive ground shots then said: 'There. What do you think? The fashion editor of *Vogue* said it was shit hot.'

'What does the badge mean?'

'It means I'm first reserve for the United Arab Emirates Olympic squad.'

184

They locked up and left the shop. Rachel was driving to Selby to visit her grandparents. It was almost a month since her return from London and though she had telephoned the Jacksons, she had been putting off the visit. She did not expect it to be cosy.

As she drove, she glanced at the glove compartment. Paul's latest postcard lay there. She had met the postman outside the flat when she was leaving for work.

'Here's another one for you,' he had said.

Even the postal authorities had tuned into the rhythm of Paul's cards. They arrived every three or four days. The latest had a picture of Karl Marx. The message on the back read:

Paul's Jazz Stories No. 485
A trumpet player touring in the Deep South had his leg bitten off by an alligator in the Everglades. He phoned the band leader. TP: An alligator bit off my leg. BL: Which one? TP: No idea. All these alligators look alike. LYM, Paul.

Rachel had replied with a picture of Bootham Bar, one of the ancient gates to the city, and the message:

Rachel's Yorkshire Folklore
Wife to husband on his death-bed: Ah'm off down t'stairs to mak a cup o' tea. If tha feels thysen slippin' away be sure to snuff t'candle out. LYF, R.'

She posted it at the box at the corner of the street where her grandparents lived. On her arrival she sat down, according to tradition, in the rocking-chair. She and her grandfather skirmished warily about her London trip.

'So you didn't get mugged then?'

'No. And nobody picked my pocket. And nobody tried to short-change me. And I spoke to several people, and they spoke to me. Mostly in English.'

'You were very lucky, flower.'

As far as Mr Jackson was concerned, London was in enemy hands. It was inhabited by thieves and con men, and administered by smooth-talking hucksters in City suits. Rachel agreed with him about the City slickers, but sniffed bias elsewhere.

'You're prejudiced,' she said.

'Me? Prejudiced? Never! I am fully prepared to go to London, and *prove* that I'm right. The day York City get to the Cup Final at Wembley, I'll be there.'

It was like a commitment to give up smoking his pipe to celebrate the abolition of income tax and he waited, eagerly, for her challenge. Rachel knew the game. She had played it many times before.

'York City? Cup Final? Wembley?'

'Check your facts. The lads got to the Semi-Final in 1955. And we should have got to the Final an' all.'

'Is that the time you were cheated? They sent a blind referee? Was that what happened?'

'You're a cheeky madam, our Rachel.' He winked at her, then added: 'But yes, that's exactly what happened.'

Mrs Jackson came in from the kitchen, with the obligatory pot of tea and the biscuit tin. She kicked her husband gently on the ankle. She was wearing soft slippers and the blow was not lethal. 'Hey, you. Off your bottom. We need cups and saucers.'

He rubbed his ankle in simulated agony, then got up and limped into the kitchen. Rachel knew that only when the three of them were decently settled in their places, each with a cup of tea, would any serious conversation be permitted. Those were the house rules. She also knew that once those conditions were fulfilled, there would be no hedging.

Mrs Jackson stirred her tea then turned to Rachel, and said abruptly: 'You found him, then?'

'Yes. I found him.'

'And did you like what you found?'

There was a cutting edge to her grandmother's voice. Her grandfather sat quietly. He was likely to remain so. Rachel knew that game too, though she had rarely played it.

'I liked him very much indeed. He's a kind man, and a generous man. He's fun to be with. I've learned a lot from

186

him already. So yes, I like him very much indeed, and given time, I'll probably get to love him too.' She hesitated, then added the footnote they all knew had to come sooner or later. 'I'd say that was pretty good, for a Jew Boy, wouldn't you?'

'That's not a fair thing to say.'

'Isn't it what you said to Mum? When she told you she was pregnant? Didn't you say: "Pity he's a Jew Boy"? And don't you owe her an apology? And me? And Paul? You owe all three of us an apology, for God's sake!'

Before his wife could reply, Mr Jackson broke in. 'Listen to me, petal. I'm not saying what we said was good or decent. But we're all prisoners of the way we were brought up. We were taught if you went off after dark, a black man might catch you. We were taught to call Catholics rat catchers. And we were taught that Jews had a lot of money and were, well, different. Like the book says, you've got to forgive us if we know not what we do.'

'But you were growing up in the Thirties, and you lived through the war. What about Hitler? What about the Holocaust? Didn't you learn anything from that? Or did you think it was newspaper talk?'

'You're the one that's learning, Rachel.'

'That's an understatement,' she said sharply.

'Don't be angry, love, just listen to me.'

And she listened to her grandfather.

'You've always thought we were a bit special. You'd come running to us when your mother wouldn't let you have your own way, and we'd *let* you have your own way. That's what grandparents are for. We can spoil our grandchildren and then hand them back when we get tired. *But* there's a moment when you discover your grandparents aren't all that special. They've got warts. They make mistakes. They do things they're ashamed of.' He hesitated but held up a hand indicating: please be quiet, I haven't finished yet. Rachel realized he was close to tears. He was dragging the thoughts out one at a time, and painfully, but he continued: 'I'm ashamed of what I said to your mother that day. By the time I'd said it, she was shouting at me and crying and such. She never forgave me for what I said, and I don't blame her. I wanted to grab the words back as soon as I'd said them, but it was too late. They must have set off from somewhere inside of me, and yes, I'm ashamed to admit it. And you're right, Rachel, I do owe you an apology. You and your mother and your father. Your *real* father, I mean. I hope this is it. The apology. There. Now you know. Your grandad isn't perfect after all. But at least I admit it. I'm sorry.'

He stood up and placed his cup of tea carefully on the mantelpiece. He hadn't drunk any of it.

'It's taken me twenty-six years to say this. And I never want to talk about any of it again.'

He left the room. They heard the back door open and close. Rachel half rose to follow him.

'Leave him,' said Mrs Jackson. 'He'll be in the back yard, having a good cry. He won't want any interruptions.'

Rachel settled back in the rocking-chair. The creak from its rockers was the only sound until eventually her grand-mother said: 'It's different today. In them days it was marriage or nothing. Nowadays they could have moved in together, like you and Will. She could have had an abortion. All things like that. More choices. When it's marriage or nothing, there's no escape.'

'Maybe that's progress.'

'Call it progress if it takes your fancy,' said Mrs Jackson with a truculent emphasis, indicating there was nothing more to be said on the subject. Rachel wanted her to say more.

'Do you still think they were better off *not* getting married?'

'I do.' The mouth was set, the mind was made up, and had been for two and a half decades. 'If you want my opinion, flower, it would have been a right disaster of a marriage. She was far better off with our John.'

'You can't be sure. You can't prove it one way or another.'

'I can't prove my case. You can't prove yours. So I might as well tell myself I was right. It's better than torturing myself. There's enough unhappiness in the world without manufacturing it in your own head.'

It was her grandmother's special brand of bedrock, peasant wisdon; there was no way of answering it, and no point in trying.

Driving back to York she pondered what had been said and, equally significant, what had been omitted. Her grandfather had apologized, at a personal cost only he could assess. Her grandmother had *not* apologized and that, too, had been a careful and conscious gesture. She would admit to confusion in a difficult and changing world. She would not admit to being wrong.

There was much more Rachel had wanted to say, so many speeches she had rehearsed in her mind. She had planned to tell them that the Holocaust was not Hitler's sole invention. It was simply the efficient and logical development of a persecution that had been refined down the centuries across the whole of Europe and beyond. Consider the geographical spread: Paul's grandparents had fled from pre-Revolutionary Russia; the word 'ghetto' had been invented in picturesque Venice; and England our England, this precious gem and land of the free, had shown an equal taste for racial blood-lust too. Her native city of York, the living theme-park beloved of American tourists, had organized its own pogrom, and its own mini-Holocaust centuries ago. It was smaller than Hitler's, only because numerically speaking York required a more modest final solution.

And all right, so we all knew that sub-species of politician that tried to keep the voters happy by giving them somebody to hate; but those ghastly seeds could not take root on stony ground. Was it kosher to use a Christian reference in the debate? What the hell – the point was dead simple. The political zealots could only get away with it because decent, ordinary, working people were able to say, 'Pity he's a Jew Boy', even in a careless moment, and even if it were instantly regretted.

All this she had intended to say to her grandparents. She

had wanted to hurt them, humiliate them, make them see what they had done. Now, looking back, she was relieved at her failure. Perhaps there had to be a statute of limitation on bitterness and revenge, if only so life could stumble on in a semblance of harmony.

All the same, she stood by every unspoken syllable. She knew she was right; and her city of York had lost some of its sweetness.

Over the days and weeks of mad March, Rachel waited for her soul to catch up. Nothing much happened. Racial identity, albeit hybrid, was a curious little number to be landed with; what the musicians at the Club Misterioso might call 'a heavy scene'. She had managed all her life without thinking about the idea of race. She was Northern English; that was enough to live by. She liked it when England beat Australia at cricket: she liked it even more when Yorkshire beat Middlesex; but if the matches were lost, she slept easily enough. It was only a game, and rather a daft game, viewed objectively.

She tried to map the changes in her personality and outlook that John had predicted, but they were tricky to handle, like spaghetti. The minute she seemed to have a new facet defined and controlled, it slid off the fork and back into the mêlée. Perhaps she was over-complicating the whole business. Looked at coldly, what had she done? She had left her York life-style behind for a week, and adjusted overnight to a different one. There were probably eight million life-styles in the naked cities of the world, and at least a thousand that would suit her.

It was like choosing a dress or a coat. You tried on half-a-dozen, but after a while it got boring, or the shop was about to close, and you settled for something less then ideal; the colour not quite right and a little too loose around the shoulders, but after all, what did you need from clothing? Warmth and protection. That was the specification.

Maybe that was what Paul meant by travelling desper-ately. He was prepared to spend a lifetime looking for the perfect style, in the certain knowledge that he would never find it. She hoped he would find something that fitted before the shop closed. She hoped she would too.

Spring arrived in the North, on or about April Fool's Day, which most people agreed was right in character. Snow-drops popped out for a quick look round and decided to stay; daffodils blossomed, but carefully; early tourists with foreign accents were glimpsed in the vicinity of the Railway Museum; the sap rose in selected areas, but missed York City football club, who once again avoided the tedium of a long trip to Wembley.

After the painful exhilaration of the visit to her grand-parents, Rachel slid back into a pre-London routine, daily sipping the mixture as before, punctuated every few days by a card from Paul. On 2 April she received one with a chirpy photograph of the young Mickey Rooney and Judy Garland. On the back was written:

Paul's (True) Jazz Stories No. 206
In 1958, Duke Ellington's Band came to England and he met H.M. the Queen. The talk went thisaway. Queen: When were you last in England? Duke: In 1933, Your Majesty, *years* before you were born. What a hero! LYM, Paul.

Rachel's reply was a subversive card drawn by Steve Bell, and the legend:

Rachel's Very Old Yorkshire Folklore
Yorkshire Bedroom Scene. Wife: Nibble my ear like when we was first wed. Husband: Hang on while I put my teeth in. LYF, R.'

The contractors started work on Will's Old People's Home. He swore he heard the site foreman instructing his men, as they dug out the trenches for the foundations: 'If you hit any Roman pavements, cover the buggers up with topsoil, before anybody notices.'

Whatever Browning's feeling about England and April,

191

the immediate consequence of half-hearted local sunshine was a rush of customers into Glenn Travel, eager to be jet-setting towards the real thing. Towards the end of a frenzied Saturday afternoon, Joan and Rachel suddenly hit a lull and fell upon it wearily and eagerly.

Joan lit a cigarette and said: 'I am totally knackered. I have never felt knackereder. How do you feel about instant dismissal, sweetheart?'

It was a familiar and well-oiled routine.

'How can I avoid instant dismissal?'

The two women spoke the answer in unison: 'Make us a cup of tea.'

They had worked together so long, and so contentedly, that the words snapped out with the synchronized fluency of vintage Abbott and Costello.

While Rachel was in the back room, making the tea, she heard an unexpected sound from the shop. Joan was laughing. It wasn't the cool professional chuckle she adopted to humour customers, even when they were driving her round every available bend. It was the real thing.

Curious to discover what was causing the laughter, she put her ear close to the door and heard a man's voice.

'Now listen carefully, lady, because I don't intend to repeat myself. I want a round-trip to Israel, no shlock, say a dollar ninety-five a day. I'd like to stay on a kibbutz with hot and cold running bagels and a nice view of the Wailing Wall. If you can throw in an LP of *Fiddler on the Roof* and a hot pastrami on rye, I think we might have ourselves a deal. What do you think?'

Rachel decided to leave tea-making for later and walked through into the shop.

'Hi, Pops,' she said to the cause of the trouble.

'My darling daughter.'

Paul leaned across the counter and kissed her hand in a cool parody of elegance. Joan stared at the performance.

'Is this who I think it is?' she asked.

'That depends who you think I am. But if you think I'm Rachel's beloved Daddy, then you are absolutely right.

You have won tonight's star prize, a dream holiday for two in Israel. And while we're on the subject, what are you doing next week?' He leered at Joan, in his modified Groucho mode.

'I'm washing my hair. All week.'

'I wouldn't bother. It looks fairly clean to me.'

He turned to Rachel, simulating anger. 'Why didn't you tell me?'

'Why didn't I tell you what?'

'Why didn't you tell me the person you work with is a vision of loveliness? A monument to pulchritude? A temple to all that is finest in womanhood.'

'Bollocks,' said Joan.

'*And* a linguist.'

After the shop had closed, Rachel and Paul walked down to the riverside. She had invited him to the flat, but he had a train to catch. He wanted to be back at the club in time to announce the final set. Rachel was puzzled by the logic, if any, of the visit, and asked: 'When did you arrive in York?'

'About twenty minutes before I walked into the shop.'

'And you're going back tonight?'

'Sure. No point in rushing these things. Besides, I wanted to grab a few slices of historical ambience.'

'Why did you come?'

'To see my daughter.'

They sat on a low stone wall overlooking the water. Small boats bounced around, rowed by resentful fathers, pressured into hiring the damn things by wives and children who had seen the Boat Race on television and figured it looked easy. The most inept of the fathers rowed very slowly and in near-perfect circles. From time to time, the entire fleet was thrown into mayhem by a passing motor launch, a property developer's status symbol on parade. The ducks, who had watched the Romans play all the same games, rode the ripples unconcerned.

'What I have to say to you,' said Paul, 'isn't the sort of thing to say on the telephone or in a letter.'

'It sounds ominous.'

'I've got some good news that might be bad, and some bad news that might be good. I can't decide which is which.'

'Tell me the news, and I'll decide which is which.'

'OK. First, Pat and I have decided to split. I think she really needs an older man. Somebody more mature.'

'That seems like bad news to me.'

'It seems like bad news to me, but I'm trying to be terribly, terribly brave.'

Briefly, he sounded like Noël Coward, before resuming his normal self. If was the genuine Paul Webster who continued: 'If I talk about it seriously, I tend to cry, and I can't bear to see a grown man cry in public, especially if it's me.'

'So what's the good news?'

'The good news is there's a job going at the club. Catering manageress, chief barmaid, public relations consultant, press officer, keeper of the candles, personal assistant to the managing director and resident psychiatrist. It's a challenging vacancy for the right candidate. By way of compensation the money's really lousy. Previous experience in a travel agency is essential.'

'And that's the good news?'

'I don't know. You tell me.'

Below them, a rowing boat headed straight towards the wall. A sweating, red-faced father flapped desperately looking for reverse as his little girl yelled: 'Daddy, you're really stupid!'

'Sounds like fair comment,' said Paul.

'Not necessarily,' said Rachel.

She asked Paul for time to think about the offer. He gave her the choice: either twenty minutes or a month. She opted for the month.

From the beginning, Will had no doubt what her decision would be.

'You'll go, won't you?'

'I don't know. I haven't decided.'

'I knew from the moment you decided to look for your

father. I knew how it would end. It would end with you going away.'

'Even if I hadn't found him?'

'You showed me that letter Paul wrote you. I think you're like his mother. The other Rachel.'

'What do you mean?'

'You're a little gypsy.'

She made a sudden discovery.

'That woman. Paul's mother. The other Rachel. Do you realize she was my grandmother?'

It was a startling new thought, bright and shiny like the pennies rich men threw to street urchins in Victorian novels. She was a direct descendant of the woman who had marched the streets, fighting Fascism; she was another little gypsy, and an associate member of the world's most resolute wandering tribe. What was Paul's phrase? Travelling desperately . . .

The days passed, until they were a week, and then two, and still they talked.

'*When* you go to London . . .'

'*If* I go to London . . .'

They competed with their emphases. The competition told its own story, because they were not competitive people.

'When you go to London,' Will persisted, 'will you see Mike?'

'Only if he's playing the club.'

'Forgive me if I say: ho hum.'

'I'm not in love with Mike Daley, or with anybody else.'

'Including me?'

'I meant anybody else in London.'

The amendment came too late and besides, they had always tried to cultivate the habit of truth. It was addictive and sometimes painful, but lies hurt more in the end.

The truth was she had never been in love with Will, much as she loved his loyal friendship. His physical presence didn't make the clichés tumble: the blood never quickened, neither did the earth move nor the breakers pound the rocky seashore. He was a sweet guy: end of message.

She had moved in with him as a gesture, a mild revolutionary response to living at home at a time of her life when, by her calculations, she should long ago have pushed herself out of the nest. She had a taste for radical gestures, even if they seemed feeble in retrospect. She had rejected university, despite her sack full of O and A levels, mainly because all her best friends, with similarly laden sacks, were *not* rejecting university. A job in a travel agency, with imperceptible career prospects, had appealed to her instincts, though she had added a gloss of reason: 'I might as well grab a job while stocks last. By the time I'm through university, jobs might have disappeared from the face of the earth.'

It was simple, old-fashioned, healthy perversity. John had argued with her, gently and benignly, but weakened his case, as always, by his obstinate determination to see the other person's point of view.

Her mother, she now saw, had understood totally and, with stray looks and thrownaway phrases, tacitly approved. She had never lost her taste for the tightrope.

The whole debate was about people's perception of tomorrow. Will and John needed to know what was going to happen tomorrow. Rachel, and her mother when young, relished the fact that tomorrow would come as a surprise, not to mention tomorrow and tomorrow. If along the way they also heard the chimes at midnight, well, wasn't that good music to live by, with a touch of the blues by way of redemption?

'Tomorrow,' said Will.

'Tomorrow.'

Her worldly goods were neatly packed, divided between the family home and the boot of the car, with a few designated morsels for remembrance to be left at the flat.

'It's all been a bit like a marriage, hasn't it?' he said.

'Maybe that's the trouble.'

196

He wanted marriage; she didn't. It was a tricky basis for living together on a permanent basis.

Rachel looked at her watch. It was almost seven o'clock and they had already eaten. That was how they had planned it: an early meal, then a leisurely final evening together, comprising Mahler, Scrabble and a bottle of their house white.

'Will,' she said.

'You want to go now?'

He had guessed right, again.

'If I stay, it's going to be awful. Like a cross between the Last Supper and *Brief Encounter*.'

'Whatever you want.'

She stood up.

'You could come with me. Have a weekend in London. I could introduce you to my father.'

He shook his head.

'I've got one or two things organized for tomorrow.'

Tomorrow was organized.

'If I go now, I should just catch the final set,' said Rachel.

ELEVEN

Milestones

The A1 was the only way to travel. The road-houses were run by people with names and children and dogs, instead of faraway boardrooms with corporate images. You might even find sugar in a bowl and sauce in a bottle. It was a decent road, with roundabouts and even the road-works looked as if men had been here with shovels and sweated a bit.

It was dusk, tending to darkness, and time for music. She slipped a cassette into the player. She knew what she would hear. She had planned it this way.

She heard Mike's voice: 'Just one more. This is for you, Rachel. Paul says it's a tune you like. I'll have to play it quietly so as not to disturb the neighbours. You can play this one when it's time to ring your bloke.'

Mike played the tune and she heard another voice. It belonged to a dark-haired man, a desperate traveller from a wandering tribe.

'"Misterioso"? It's a piece of music. A blues, naturally, like all my best friends. Written by Thelonious Monk. Piano player, full name – Thelonious Sphere Monk. If you're a musician, you'll understand me when I say it's a blues built around walking sixths. If you're not a musician, let me offer my congratulations and tell you "Misterioso" is a tune that haunts you. Always beyond reach. Just around the corner. A sweet promise and the echo of a sad dream.'

Then she said to herself: 'Sorry Pops, but it still sounds to me like it could be a really good gig.'